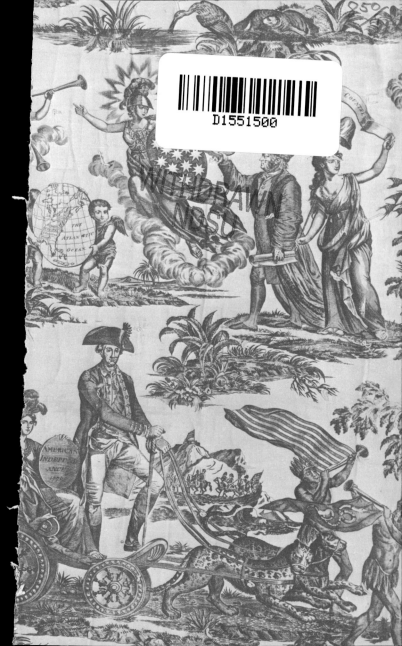

THE BAGATELLES
FROM PASSY

THE BAGATELLES
FROM PASSY

BY

BENJAMIN FRANKLIN 1706-1790.

———

*Written by him in French and English
and printed on his own Press at Paris
while he was America's first Minister
Plenipotentiary to the Court of France*

———

TEXT AND FACSIMILE

The Eakins Press, New York, Publishers

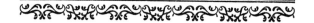

CONTENTS

THE ELYSIAN FIELDS

PARABLE AGAINST PERSECUTION

TO THE ROYAL ACADEMY OF * * * * *

A TALE

INFORMATION TO THOSE WHO
WOULD REMOVE TO AMERICA

An essay on the realities and opportunities of life in America, to correct the false ideas of French persons, especially those of the leisure class, who might think America was a never-never land where they would be honored for being well born.

THE EPHEMERA

An emblem of human life, an allegory of time and space, written to Madame Brillon and sent to her after they had spent a summer afternoon together strolling on an island in the Seine and watching May Flies.

THE PHILOSOPHER AND THE GOUT

A fable in verse composed by Madame Brillon for Mr. F., (the only Bagatelle he printed not written by himself).

DIALOGUE BETWEEN THE GOUT
AND MR. FRANKLIN

A conversation between the sufferer and his sickness, set down for Madame Brillon, in which The Gout tries to

BACKGROUND AND NOTES

ix

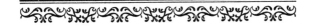

REMARKS
ON THE POLITENESS
OF THE SAVAGES
OF NORTH AMERICA

SAVAGES we call them, because their manners differ from ours, which we think the Perfection of Civility; they think the same of theirs.

Perhaps if we could examine the manners of different Nations with Impartiality, we should find no People so rude as to be without any Rules of Politeness; nor any so polite as not to have some remains of Rudeness.

The Indian Men, when young, are Hunters and Warriors; when old, Counsellors; for all their Government is by the Counsel or Advice of the Sages; there is no Force, there are no Prisons, no Officers to compel Obedience, or inflict Punishment. Hence they generally study Oratory; the best Speaker having the most Influence. The Indian Women till the Ground, dress the Food, nurse and bring up the Children, and preserve and hand down to Posterity the Memory of Public Transactions. These Em-

1

ployments of Men and Women are accounted natural and honorable. Having few Artificial Wants, they have abundance of Leisure for Improvement by Conversation. Our laborious manner of Life compared with theirs, they esteem slavish and base; and the Learning on which we value ourselves; they regard as frivolous and useless. An Instance of this occurred at the Treaty of Lancaster in Pennsylvania, Anno 1744, between the Government of Virginia & the Six Nations. After the principal Business was settled, the Commissioners from Virginia acquainted the Indians by a Speech, that there was at Williamsburg a College with a Fund for Educating Indian Youth, and that if the Chiefs of the Six-Nations would send down half a dozen of their Sons to that College, the Government would take Care that they should be well provided for, and instructed in all the Learning of the white People. It is one of the Indian Rules of Politeness not to answer a public Proposition the same day that it is made; they think it would be treating it as a light Matter; and that they show it Respect by taking time to consider it, as of a Matter important. They therefore deferred their Answer till the day following; when their Speaker began by expressing their deep Sense of the Kindness of the Virginia Government, in making them that Offer; for we know, says he, that you highly esteem the kind of Learning taught in those Colleges, and that the Maintenance of our Young Men while with you, would be very expensive to you. We are convinced therefore that you mean to do us good by your Proposal, and we thank you heartily. But you who are wise must know, that different Nations have different Conceptions of things; and you will therefore not take it amiss, if our Ideas of this Kind of Education happen not to be the same with yours. We have had some Experience of it: Several of our Young People were formerly brought up at the Colleges of the Northern Provinces; they were instructed in all your Sciences; but when they came back to us, they were bad Runners, ignorant of every means of living in the Woods, unable to bear either Cold or Hunger, knew neither how to build a Cabin, take a Deer, or kill an Enemy, spoke our Language imperfectly; were therefore neither fit for Hunters, Warriors, or Counsellors; they were totally good for nothing. We are however not the less obliged by your kind Offer, tho' we decline accepting it; and to show our grateful Sense of it, if the Gentlemen of Virginia will send us a dozen of their Sons, we will take great Care of their Education, instruct them in all we know, and make *Men* of them.

Having frequent Occasions to hold public Councils, they have acquired great Order and Decency in conducting them. The old Men sit in the foremost Ranks, the Warriors in the next, and the Women and Children in the hindmost. The Business of the Women is to take exact notice of what passes, imprint it in their Memories, for they have no Writing, and communicate it to their Children. They are the Records of the Council, and they preserve Tradition of the Stipulations in Treaties a hundred Years back, which when we compare with our Writings we always find exact. He that would speak, rises. The rest observe a profound Silence. When he has finished and sits down, they leave him five or six Minutes to recollect, that if he has omitted any thing he intended to say, or has any thing to add, he may rise again and deliver it. To interrupt another, even in common Conversation, is reckoned highly indecent. How different this is from the Conduct of a polite British House of Commons, where scarce a Day passes without some Confusion that makes the Speaker hoarse in calling *to order*; and how different from the mode of Conversation in many polite Companies of Europe, where if you do not deliver your Sentence with great Rapidity, you are cut off in the middle of it by the impatient Loquacity of those you converse with, & never suffer'd to finish it.

The Politeness of these Savages in Conversation is indeed carried to excess, since it does not permit them to contradict, or deny the Truth of what is asserted in their Presence. By this means

4

they indeed avoid Disputes, but then it becomes difficult to know their Minds, or what Impression you make upon them. The Missionaries who have attempted to convert them to Christianity, all complain of this as one of the great Difficulties of their Mission. The Indians hear with Patience the Truths of the Gospel explained to them, and give their usual Tokens of Assent and Approbation: you would think they were convinced. No such Matter. It is mere Civility.

A Swedish Minister having assembled the Chiefs of the Sasquehanah Indians, made a Sermon to them, acquainting them with the principal historical Facts on which our Religion is founded, such as the Fall of our first Parents by Eating an Apple, the Coming of Christ to repair the Mischief, his Miracles and Suffering, &c. When he had finished, an Indian Orator stood up to thank him. What you have told us, says he, is all very good. It is indeed bad to eat Apples. It is better to make them all into Cyder. We are much obliged by your Kindness in coming so far to tell us those things which you have heard from your Mothers. In Return I will tell you some of those we have heard from ours.

In the Beginning our Fathers had only the Flesh of Animals to subsist on, and if their Hunting was unsuccessful, they were starving. Two of our young Hunters having killed a Deer,

made a Fire in the Woods to broil some Parts of
it. When they were about to satisfy their Hunger, they beheld a beautiful young Woman descend from the Clouds, and seat herself on that
Hill which you see yonder among the blue
Mountains. They said to each other, it is a Spirit
that perhaps has smelt our broiling Venison, &
wishes to eat of it: let us offer some to her. They
presented her with the Tongue: She was pleased
with the Taste of it, & said, your Kindness shall
be rewarded. Come to this Place after thirteen
Moons, and you shall find something that will
be of great Benefit in nourishing you and your
Children to the latest Generations. They did so,
and to their Surprise found Plants they had never
seen before, but which from that ancient time
have been constantly cultivated among us to our
great Advantage. Where her right Hand had
touch'd the Ground, they found Maize; where
her left Hand had touch'd it, they found Kidney-
beans; and where her Backside had sat on it, they
found Tobacco. The good Missionary, disgusted
with this idle Tale, said, what I delivered to you
were sacred Truths: but what you tell me is
mere Fable, Fiction & Falsehood. The Indian
offended, reply'd, my Brother, it seems your
Friends have not done you Justice in your Education; they have not well instructed you in the
Rules of common Civility. You saw that we who
understand and practise those Rules, believed all

6

your Stories; why do you refuse to believe ours?

When any of them come into our Towns, our People are apt to croud round them, gaze upon them, and incommode them where they desire to be private; this they esteem great Rudeness, and the Effect of want of Instruction in the Rules of Civility and good Manners. We have, say they, as much curiosity as you, and when you come into our Towns we wish for Opportunities of looking at you; but for this purpose we hide ourselves behind Bushes where you are to pass, and never intrude ourselves into your Company.

Their Manner of entring one anothers Villages has likewise its Rules. It is reckon'd uncivil in travelling Strangers to enter a Village abruptly, without giving Notice of their Approach. Therefore as soon as they arrive within hearing, they stop and hollow, remaining there till invited to enter. Two old Men usually come out to them, and lead them in. There is in every Village a vacant Dwelling, called the Strangers House. Here they are placed, while the old Men go round from Hut to Hut acquainting the Inhabitants that Strangers are arrived, who are probably hungry and weary; and every one sends them what he can spare of Victuals and Skins to repose on. When the Strangers are refresh'd, Pipes & Tobacco are brought; and then, but not before, Conversation begins, with Enquiries who they are, whither bound, what

7

News, &c. and it usually ends with Offers of Service, if the Strangers have Occasion of Guides or any Necessaries for continuing their Journey; and nothing is exacted for the Entertainment.

The same Hospitality, esteemed among them as a principal Virtue, is practised by private Persons; of which *Conrad Weiser*, our Interpreter, gave me the following Instance. He had been naturaliz'd among the Six-Nations, and spoke well the Mohock Language. In going thro' the Indian Country, to carry a Message from our Governor to the Council at *Onondaga*, he called at the Habitation of *Canassetego*, an old Acquaintance, who embraced him, spread Furs for him to sit on, placed before him some boiled Beans and Venison, and mixed some Rum and Water for his Drink. When he was well refresh'd, and had lit his Pipe, Canassetego began to converse with him, ask'd how he had fared the many Years since they had seen each other, whence he then came, what occasioned the Journey, &c. &c. Conrad answered all his Questions; and when the Discourse began to flag, the Indian, to continue it, said, Conrad, you have liv'd long among the white People, and know something of their Customs; I have been sometimes at Albany, and have observed that once in seven Days, they shut up their Shops and assemble all in the great House; tell me, what it is for? what do they do there? They meet there, says Conrad,

8

to hear & learn *good things*. I do not doubt, says
the Indian, that they tell you so; they have told
me the same; but I doubt the Truth of what they
say, & I will tell you my Reasons. I went lately
to Albany to sell my Skins, & buy Blankets,
Knives, Powder, Rum, &c. You know I used
generally to deal with Hans Hanson; but I was a
little inclined this time to try some other Merchants. However I called first upon Hans, and
ask'd him what he would give for Beaver; He
said he could not give more than four Shillings a
Pound; but, says he, I cannot talk on Business
now; this is the Day when we meet together to
learn *good things*, and I am going to the Meeting. So I thought to myself since I cannot do any
Business to day, I may as well go to the Meeting
too; and I went with him. There stood up a Man
in black, and began to talk to the People very
angrily. I did not understand what he said; but
perceiving that he looked much at me, & at Hanson, I imagined he was angry at seeing me there;
so I went out, sat down near the House, struck
Fire & lit my Pipe; waiting till the Meeting
should break up. I thought too, that the Man
had mentioned something of Beaver, and I suspected it might be the Subject of their Meeting.
So when they came out I accosted my Merchant;
well Hans, says I, I hope you have agreed to
give more than four Shillings a Pound. No, says
he, I cannot give so much. I cannot give more

9

than three Shillings and six Pence. I then spoke to several other Dealers, but they all sung the same Song, three & six Pence, three & six Pence. This made it clear to me that my Suspicion was right; and that whatever they pretended of Meeting to learn *good things*, the real Purpose was to consult, how to cheat Indians in the Price of Beaver. Consider but a little, Conrad, and you must be of my Opinion. If they met so often to learn *good things*, they would certainly have learnt some before this time. But they are still ignorant. You know our Practice. If a white Man in travelling thro' our Country, enters one of our Cabins, we all treat him as I treat you; we dry him if he is wet, we warm him if he is cold, and give him Meat & Drink that he may allay his Thirst and Hunger, & we spread soft Furs for him to rest & sleep on: We demand nothing in return*. But if I go into a white Man's House at Albany, and ask for Victuals & Drink, they

---

* *It is remarkable that in all Ages and Countries, Hospitality has been allowed as the Virtue of those, whom the civiliz'd were pleased to call Barbarians; the Greeks celebrated the Scythians for it. The Saracens possess'd it eminently; and it is to this day the reigning Virtue of the wild Arabs. S. Paul too, in the Relation of his Voyage & Shipwreck, on the Island of Melita, says,* The Barbarous People shew'd us no little Kindness; for they kindled a Fire, and received us every one, because of the present Rain & because of the Cold.

say, where is your Money? and if I have none, they say, get out, you Indian Dog. You see they have not yet learnt those little *good things*, that we need no Meetings to be instructed in, because our Mothers taught them to us when we were Children. And therefore it is impossible their Meetings should be as they say for any such purpose, or have any such Effect; they are only to contrive *the Cheating of Indians in the Price of Beaver*.

BILKED FOR BREAKFAST

MR. FRANKLIN

TO MADAME LA FRETÉ

Upon my word, you did well, Madam, not to come so far, at so inclement a Season, only to find so wretched a Breakfast. My Son & I were not so wise. I will tell you the Story.

As the Invitation was for eleven O'clock, & you were of the Party, I imagined I should find a substantial Breakfast; that there would be a large Company; that we should have not only Tea, but Coffee, Chocolate, perhaps a Ham, & several other good Things. I resolved to go on Foot; my Shoes were a little too tight; I arrived almost lamed. On entering the Courtyard, I was a little surprised to find it so empty of Carriages, & to see that we were the first to arrive. We go up the Stairs. Not a Sound. We enter the Breakfast Room. No one except the Abbé & Monsieur Cabanis. Breakfast over, & eaten! Nothing on the Table except a few Scraps of Bread & a little Butter. General astonishment; a Servant sent running to tell Madame Helvétius that we have come for Breakfast. She leaves her toilet

Table; she enters with her Hair half dressed. It is declared surprising that I have come, when you wrote me that you would not come. I Deny it. To prove it, they show me your Letter, which they have received and kept.

Finally another Breakfast is ordered. One Servant runs for fresh Water, another for Coals. The Bellows are plied with a will. I was very Hungry; it was so late; "a watched pot is slow to boil," as Poor Richard says. Madame sets out for Paris & leaves us. We begin to eat. The Butter is soon finished. The Abbé asks if we want more. Yes, of course. He rings. No one comes. We talk; he forgets the Butter. I began scraping the Dish; at that he seizes it & runs to the Kitchen for some. After a while he comes slowly back, saying mournfully that there is no more of it in the House. To entertain me the Abbé proposes a Walk; my feet refuse. And so we give up Breakfast; & we go upstairs to his apartment to let his good Books furnish the end of our Repast—.

I am left utterly disconsolate, having, instead of half a Dozen of your sweet, affectionate, substantial, & heartily applied Kisses, which I expected from your Charity, having received only the Shadow of one given by Madame Helvétius, willingly enough, it is true, but the lightest & most superficial kiss that can possibly be imagined.

13

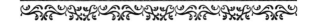

THE FLIES

TO MADAME HELVÉTIUS

THE Flies of the Apartments of Mr. Franklin request Permission to present their Respects to Madame Helvétius, & to express in their best Language their Gratitude for the Protection which she has been kind enough to give them,

Bizz izzzz ouizz a ouizzzz izzzzzzzz, &c.

We have long lived under the hospitable Roof of the said Good Man Franklin. He has given us free Lodgings; we have also eaten & drunk the whole Year at his Expense without its having cost us anything. Often, when his Friends & he have emptied a Bowl of Punch, he has left us a sufficient Quantity to intoxicate a hundred of us Flies. We have drunk freely of it, & after that we have made our Sallies, our Circles & our Cotillions very prettily in the Air of his Room, & have gaily consummated our little Loves under his Nose. In short, we should have been the happiest People in the World, if he had not permitted a Number of our declared Enemies to remain at the top of his Wainscoting, where they spread their Nets to catch us, & tore us pitilessly to pieces. People of a Disposition both subtle & ferocious, abominable Combination! You, most excellent Woman, had the goodness to order that all these Assassins with their Habitations & their Snares should be swept away; & your Orders (as they always ought to be) were carried out immediately. Since that Time we live happily, & we enjoy the Beneficence of the said Good Man Franklin without fear.

One Thing alone remains for us to wish in order to assure the Permanence of our Good Fortune; permit us to say it,

Bizz izzzz ouizz a ouizzzz izzzzzzzz, &c.

It is to see the two of you henceforth forming a single Household.

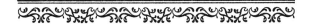

THE ELYSIAN FIELDS

MR. FRANKLIN

TO MADAME HELVÉTIUS

Lᴀsᴛ Night I retir'd to my Chamber much shaken at the cruel Resolve, which you had just unequivocally declar'd, that you would continue single the Remainder of your Life, out of Respect for the memory of your Husband. I threw myself on my couch; &, dreaming I had died, found myself transported to the Elysian Fields. I was asked, if there was Anyone in particular that I wish'd to see?—Take me where there are Philosophers!—Two make their homes here in this garden; they are Neighbors & the best of Friends.—And who may they be?—Socrates and Helvétius.—It is with the highest Esteem that I regard them both; but let me see Helvétius first, for I understand a little French, but not a Word of Greek.

He receiv'd me most courteously, my Name & Reputation having, he said, been long familiar to him. He ask'd a thousand Questions about the War, and the present State of Religion, Liberty, & the Government of France.—But you do not

16

ask after your cherish'd Madame Helvétius; for her Part, she still loves you most devotedly;—it was in fact, no more than an Hour ago that I was in her Company.—Ah, he sigh'd, these are Memories of a happy time long past, that you bring back to me. But to achieve Happiness here, one must forget the Past. The first few Years, I thought of no one but her. But presently I found Consolation. I took another Wife, as like the first as it was possible to find. She is not, it is true, quite so beautiful; but she has as great a Fund of good Sense; she is more vivacious,— and besides, she loves me infinitely. Her continual Study is to please me: just now, she actually is out gathering with her own hand the choicest Nectar & Ambrosia, to make me a Feast this Evening. Remain here a While, and you will meet her.

Ah Sir, said I, I perceive now that your Widow is more faithful than you are; for she has had many excellent Proposals of Marriage, and she has refus'd them all. I must confess to you, that I myself have lov'd her to Distraction; but she was obdurate to my Pleadings, and rejected me flatly, because of her Love for you.

Sir, he said, you have my Sympathies indeed; for she is, in Truth, an excellent Woman, beautiful and amiable. But the Abbé de la Roche, and the Abbé Morellet, do they not still continue to visit her?—Most certainly they do; for she has

17

not lost a single one of your old Friends.—You would have been, perhaps, more successful, if (with the Bribe of some excellent Coffee & Cream) you had won over the Abbé Morellet to parley for you: for he is as subtle a Logician, as Duns Scotus or St. Thomas; he phrases his arguments so skillfully, that they become pretty nearly irrefutable. And if, (by the Gift of some fine edition of an old Classic), you had won over the Abbé de la Roche, to talk *against* you, that would have been better still; for I have always notic'd, that when his Advice to her was to follow one Course, she was mightily tempted to do the Reverse. At these Words, bearing the Nectar she had gather'd, enter'd the second Mme. Helvétius. At once I recogniz'd her to be Mrs. Franklin, my dear departed American Wife. I reclaim'd her, whereupon she answer'd coldly: I made you a good Wife for forty-nine Years & four Months—almost half a Century; let that content you. Here I have contracted a new Union, that will last all Eternity.

Mortify'd by this Rejection of my Euridice, I immediately resolv'd to quit those ungrateful Shades, & return to this good World, to see the Sun, and you. Madam, here I am! *Let us avenge ourselves!*

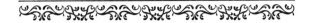

PARABLE

AGAINST PERSECUTION

IN IMITATION OF
THE LANGUAGE OF THE BIBLE

AND it came to pass after these Things, that Abraham sat in the Door of his Tent, about the going down of the Sun.

2. And behold a Man, bowed with Age, came from the Way of the Wilderness, leaning on a Staff.

3. And Abraham arose and met him, and said unto him, Turn in, I pray thee, and wash thy Feet, and tarry all Night, and thou shalt arise early on the Morrow, and go on thy Way.

4. And the Man said, Nay, for I will abide under this Tree.

5. But Abraham pressed him greatly; so he turned, and they went into the Tent; and Abraham baked unleavend Bread, and they did eat.

6. And when Abraham saw that the Man blessed not God, he said unto him, Wherefore dost thou not worship the most high God, Creator of Heaven and Earth?

19

7. And the Man answered and said, I do not worship the God thou speakest of; neither do I call upon his Name; for I have made to myself a God, which abideth alway in mine House, and provideth me with all Things.

8. And Abraham's Zeal was kindled against the Man; and he arose, and fell upon him, and drove him forth with Blows into the Wilderness.

9. And at Midnight God called unto Abraham, saying, Abraham, where is the Stranger?

10. And Abraham answered and said, Lord, he would not worship thee, neither would he call upon thy Name; therefore have I driven him out from before my Face into the Wilderness.

11. And God said, Have I born with him these hundred ninety and eight Years, and nourished him, and cloathed him, notwithstanding his Rebellion against me, and couldst not thou, that art thyself a Sinner, bear with him one Night?

12. And Abraham said, Let not the Anger of my Lord wax hot against his Servant. Lo, I have sinned; forgive me, I pray Thee:

13. And Abraham arose and went forth into the Wilderness, and sought diligently for the Man, and found him, and returned with him to his Tent; and when he had entreated him kindly, he sent him away on the Morrow with Gifts.

14. And God spake again unto Abraham, saying, For this thy Sin shall thy Seed be afflicted four Hundred Years in a strange Land:

15. But for thy Repentance will I deliver them; and they shall come forth with Power, and with Gladness of Heart, and with much Substance.

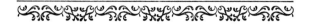

TO THE

ROYAL ACADEMY

OF * * * * *

GENTLEMEN, I have perused your late mathematical Prize Question, proposed in lieu of one in Natural Philosophy, for the ensuing year, viz. *"Any figure being given, inscribe in it as many times as possible any other smaller figure, which is also given"*. I was glad to find by these following Words, *"the Academy is of the opinion that this discovery, by extending the bounds of our knowledge, would not be without UTILITY"*, that you esteem *Utility* an essential Point in your Enquiries, which has not always been the case with all Academies; and I conclude therefore that you have given this Question instead of a philosophical, or as the Learned express it, a physical one, because you could not at the time think of a physical one that promis'd greater *Utility*.

Permit me then humbly to propose one of that sort for your consideration, and through you, if you approve it, for the serious Enquiry of learned

Physicians, Chemists, &c. of this enlightened Age.

It is universally well known, That in digesting our common Food, there is created or produced in the Bowels of human Creatures, a great Quantity of Wind.

That the permitting this Air to escape and mix with the Atmosphere, is usually offensive to the Company, from the fetid Smell that accompanies it.

That all well-bred People therefore, to avoid giving such Offence, forcibly restrain the Efforts of Nature to discharge that Wind.

That so retain'd contrary to Nature, it not only gives frequently great present Pain, but occasions future Diseases, such as habitual Cholics, Ruptures, Tympanies, &c. often destructive of the Constitution, & sometimes of Life itself.

Were it not for the odiously offensive Smell accompanying such Escapes, polite People would probably be under no more Restraint in discharging such Wind in Company, than they are in spitting, or in blowing their Noses.

My Prize Question therefore should be, *To discover some Drug wholesome & not disagreable, to be mix'd with our common Food, or Sauces, that shall render the natural Discharges of Wind from our Bodies, not only inoffensive, but agreable as Perfumes.*

That this is not a chimerical Project, and al-

together impossible, may appear from these
Considerations. That we already have some
Knowledge of Means capable of *Varying* that
Smell. He that dines on stale Flesh, especially
with much Addition of Onions, shall be able to
afford a Stink that no Company can tolerate;
while he that has lived for some Time on Vegetables only, shall have that Breath so pure as to
be insensible to the most delicate Noses; and if
he can manage so as to avoid the Report, he may
any where give Vent to his Griefs, unnoticed.
But as there are many to whom an entire Vegetable Diet would be inconvenient, and as a little
Quick-Lime thrown into a Jakes will correct the
amazing Quantity of fetid Air arising from the
vast Mass of putrid Matter contain'd in such
Places, and render it rather pleasing to the Smell,
who knows but that a little Powder of Lime (or
some other thing equivalent) taken in our Food,
or perhaps a Glass of Limewater drank at Dinner, may have the same Effect on the Air produc'd
in and issuing from our Bowels? This is worth
the Experiment. Certain it is also that we have
the Power of changing by slight Means the
Smell of another Discharge, that of our Water.
A few Stems of Asparagus eaten, shall give our
Urine a disagreable Odour; and a Pill of Turpentine no bigger than a Pea, shall bestow on it the
pleasing Smell of Violets. And why should it be
thought more impossible in Nature, to find

Means of making a Perfume of our *Wind* than of our *Water*?

For the Encouragement of this Enquiry, (from the immortal Honour to be reasonably expected by the Inventor) let it be considered of how small Importance to Mankind, or to how small a Part of Mankind have been useful those Discoveries in Science that have heretofore made Philosophers famous. Are there twenty Men in Europe at this Day, the happier, or even the easier, for any Knowledge they have pick'd out of Aristotle? What Comfort can the Vortices of Descartes give to a Man who has Whirlwinds in his Bowels! The Knowledge of Newton's mutual *Attraction* of the Particles of Matter, can it afford Ease to him who is rack'd by their mutual *Repulsion*, and the cruel Distensions it occasions? The Pleasure arising to a few Philosophers, from seeing, a few Times in their Life, the Threads of Light untwisted, and separated by the Newtonian Prism into seven Colours, can it be compared with the Ease and Comfort every Man living might feel seven times a Day, by discharging freely the Wind from his Bowels? Especially if it be converted into a Perfume: For the Pleasures of one Sense being little inferior to those of another, instead of pleasing the *Sight* he might delight the *Smell* of those about him, & make Numbers happy, which to a benevolent Mind must afford infinite Satisfaction. The generous

Soul, who now endeavours to find out whether the Friends he entertains like best Claret or Burgundy, Champagne or Madeira, would then enquire also whether they chose Musk or Lilly, Rose or Bergamot, and provide accordingly. And surely such a Liberty of *Ex-pressing* one's *Scent-iments*, and *pleasing one another*, is of infinitely more Importance to human Happiness than that Liberty of the *Press*, or of *abusing one another*, which the English are so ready to fight & die for. —In short, this Invention, if compleated, would be, as *Bacon* expresses it, *bringing Philosophy home to Mens Business and Bosoms*. And I cannot but conclude, that in Comparison therewith, for *universal* and *continual UTILITY*, the Science of the Philosophers abovementioned, even with the Addition, Gentlemen, of your *"Figure quelconque"* and the Figures inscrib'd in it, are, all together, scarcely worth a

FART-HING.

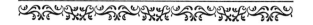

A TALE

THERE was once an Officer, a worthy man, named Montrésor, who was very ill. His parish Priest, thinking he would die, advised him to make his Peace with God, so that he would be received into Paradise. "I don't feel much Uneasiness on that Score," said Montrésor; "for last Night I had a Vision which set me entirely at rest." "What Vision did you have?" asked the good Priest. "I was," he said, "at the Gate of Paradise with a Crowd of People who wanted to enter. And St. Peter asked each of them what Religion he belonged to. One answered, 'I am a Roman Catholic.' 'Very well,' said St. Peter; 'come in, & take your Place over there among the Catholics.' Another said he belonged to the Anglican Church. 'Very well,' said St. Peter; 'come in, & take your Place over there among the Anglicans.' Another said he was a Quaker. 'Very well,' said St. Peter; 'come in, & take a Place among the Quakers.' Finally he asked me what my Religion was. 'Alas!' I replied, 'unfortunately, poor Jacques Montrésor belongs to none at all.' 'That's a pity,' said the Saint. 'I don't know where to put you but come in anyway; just find a Place for yourself wherever you can.'"

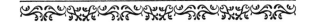

THE EPHEMERA

AN EMBLEM OF HUMAN LIFE

TRANSLATOR'S NOTE: *Madame Brillon is a very amiable Lady, and one who has a distinguished talent for Music; she lives at Passy where she moves in the same society as Mr. Franklin. In the summer of 1778 they had passed a day together at the* Moulin-Joly, *where on the same day there hovered over the river a swarm of those small flies called Ephemerae, which people call May Flies. Mr. Franklin studied them with care, and the next day sent Madame Brillon the letter of which this is the translation:*

You may remember my dear friend that when we passed that happy day together, in the delightful garden and sweet society of the *Moulin-Joly*, I stopt a little in one of our Walks, and staid some time behind the Company.

We had been shown numberless skeletons of a kind of little Fly, called an *Ephemera*, all whose successive generations we were told were bred, and expired within the day. I happened to see a living Company of them on a leaf, who appeared to be engaged in Conversation.

You know I understand all the inferior animal Tongues. My too great application to the Study of them, is the best excuse I can give for the little progress I have made in your charming language. I listened with curiosity to the discourse of these little creatures, but as they in their national vivacity spoke three or four together, I could make but little of their conversation. I found however by some broken expressions that I caught now and then, they were disputing warmly the merit of two foreign Musicians, one a Coûsin & the other a Musketo; in which dispute they spent their time seemingly as regardless of the shortness of life as if they had been sure of living a Month. Happy People, thought I! You live certainly under a wise, just and mild Government, since You have no public greivances to complain of, nor any subject of contention but the perfection or imperfection of foreign Music.

I turned from them to an Old Grey-headed one, who was single on another leaf, and talking to himself. Being amused with his soliloquy, I have put it down in writing, in hopes it will likewise amuse Her I am so much indebted to, for the most pleasing of all amusements, her delicious company, and her heavenly Harmony.

"It was," says He, "the opinion of learned

"Philosophers of our race, who lived and flour-
"ished long before my time, that this vast world[1]
"could not itself subsist more than 18 hours, and
"I think there was some Foundation for that
"opinion, since by the apparent Motion of the
"great Luminary that gives life to all Nature,
"and which in my time has evidently declined
"considerably towards the Ocean[2] at the end of
"our Earth, it must soon finish it's course, and
"be extinguished in the Waters that surround
"us, leaving the World in cold and darkness,
"necessarily producing universal death and de-
"struction. I have lived seven of those hours, a
"great age, being no less than 420 minutes of
"time! How very few of us continue so long! I
"have seen generations born, flourish and ex-
"pire. My present friends are the Children and
"Grandchildren of the friends of my Youth, who
"are now alas no more! And I must soon follow
"them, for by the course of Nature, though still
"in health, I cannot expect to live above 7 or 8
"minutes longer. What now avails all my toil
"and labor in amassing Honey-dew on this leaf,
"which I cannot live to enjoy! What the political
"struggles I have been in, or my philosophical
"studies for the benefit of our race in general!
"for in Politics, what can Law do without Mor-

1 The Moulin-Joly
2 The River Seine

30

"als?[3] Our present race of *Ephemerae* will in a
"course of minutes become corrupt like those of
"other and elder Bushes, and consequently as
"wretched. And in Philosophy, how small our
"progress! Alas, Art is long, and Life short![4]
"My friends would comfort me with the idea of a
"Name they say I shall leave behind me, and they
"tell me I have lived long enough to Nature and
"to Glory. But what will fame be to an *Ephemera*
"who no longer exists? And what will become of
"all History, in the 10 hours when the World it-
"self, even the whole *Moulin-Joly*, shall come to
"it's end, and be buried in universal ruin? After
"all my eager pursuits, no solid pleasure now
"remains, but the reflection of a long life spent
"in meaning well, the sensible conversation of a
"few Lady *Ephemerae*, and now and then a kind
"smile, and a tune from the ever amiable *Bril-
"liante*."

---

3 Quid leges fine moribus? HORACE
4 Hippocrates

THE PHILOSOPHER
AND THE GOUT

BY MADAME BRILLON

The Gout, a fearful plague without a cure,
Took lodging in a sage and felt quite sure
Of making him despair. He *did* complain,
(Wisdom can't help too much when you're in pain.
You just don't listen)—but in the end
Wisdom won out. My philosophic friend
Started to reason suavely with his Gout.
Each tried to win a philosophic bout.
"Dear Doctor," said the Gout. "You must agree
Prudence is not your strongest point. I see
You eat too much, you pass the time with dames,
You hate to take a walk; your long chess games,
Your drinking and flirtations take up time
And dissipate your powers—it's a crime.
In stopping this I'm doing you a favor.
You should say, 'Thanks, friend. You're a life-
	saver!' "

The sage asserted: "Love can do no wrong
And, softening stern Reason, keeps us young.
I love, I've always loved, I'll always be in love.

32

And someone still loves me. Heavens above!
Am I to pass my days in dull privation?
No, no. Wisdom must always rest
In relishing the gifts wherein we're blessed.
A glass of punch, a pretty mistress, maybe two
Or three or four—my wife forgave me, why
   don't you?
Any fair lady I can still delight
Shall not escape me while I stand upright.
Success in chess makes the game amusing,
But I lose interest quickly when I'm losing.
The fool renounces pleasures undiminished.
The wise man gives the game up when it's finished."

DIALOGUE
BETWEEN THE GOUT
AND MR. FRANKLIN

MIDNIGHT, OCTOBER 22, 1780

MR. F.

Eʜ! oh! eh! What have I done to merit these cruel sufferings?

THE GOUT

Many things; you have ate and drank too freely, and too much indulged those legs of yours in their indolence.

MR. F.

Who is it that accuses me?

THE GOUT

It is I, even I, the Gout.

MR. F.

What! my enemy in person?

THE GOUT

No, not your enemy.

34

Dialogue Between The Gout and Mr. F.

Mr. F.

I repeat it, my enemy; for you would not only
torment my body to death, but ruin my good
name; you reproach me as a glutton and a tip-
pler; now all the world, that knows me, will
allow that I am neither the one nor the other.

The Gout

The world may think as it pleases; it is always
very complaisant to itself, and sometimes to its
friends; but I very well know that the quantity
of meat and drink proper for a man who takes a
reasonable degree of exercise, would be too
much for another who never takes any.

Mr. F.

I take—eh! oh!—as much exercise—eh!—as I
can, Madam Gout. You know my sedentary state,
and on that account, it would seem, Madam
Gout, as if you might spare me a little, seeing it
is not altogether my own fault.

The Gout

Not a jot; your rhetoric and your politeness are
thrown away; your apology avails nothing. If
your situation in life is a sedentary one, your
amusements, your recreation, at least, should be
active. You ought to walk or ride; or, if the
weather prevents that, play at billiards. But let
us examine your course of life. While the morn-
ings are long, and you have leisure to go abroad,

what do you do? Why, instead of gaining an appetite for breakfast by salutary exercise, you amuse yourself with books, pamphlets, or newspapers, which commonly are not worth the reading. Yet you eat an inordinate breakfast, four dishes of tea with cream, and one or two buttered toasts, with slices of hung beef, which I fancy are not things the most easily digested. Immediately afterwards you sit down to write at your desk, or converse with persons who apply to you on business. Thus the time passes till one, without any kind of bodily exercise. But all this I could pardon, in regard, as you say, to your sedentary condition. But what is your practice after dinner? Walking in the beautiful gardens of those friends with whom you have dined would be the choice of men of sense; yours is to be fixed down to chess, where you are found engaged for two or three hours! This is your perpetual recreation, which is the least eligible of any for a sedentary man, because, instead of accelerating the motion of the fluids, the rigid attention it requires helps to retard the circulation and obstruct internal secretions. Wrapt in the speculations of this wretched game, you destroy your constitution. What can be expected from such a course of living but a body replete with stagnant humours, ready to fall a prey to all kinds of dangerous maladies, if I, the Gout, did not occasionally bring you relief by agitating those humours, and so purifying or dissipating them? If it was in some nook or alley in Paris, deprived of walks, that you played a while at chess after dinner, this might be excusable; but the same taste prevails with you in Passy, Auteuil, Montmartre, or Sanoy, places where there are the finest gardens and walks, a pure air, beautiful women, and most agreeable and instructive conversation: all which you might enjoy by frequenting the walks. But these are rejected for this abominable game of chess. Fie, then, Mr. Franklin! But amidst my instructions, I had almost forgot to administer my wholesome corrections; so take that twinge —and that.

Mr. F.

Oh! eh! oh! ohhh! As much instruction as you please, Madam Gout, and as many reproaches; but pray, Madam, a truce with your corrections!

The Gout

No, Sir, no, I will not abate a particle of what is so much for your good—therefore——

Mr. F.

Oh! ehhh!—It is not fair to say I take no exercise, when I do very often, going out to dine and returning in my carriage.

The Gout

That, of all imaginable exercises, is the most

slight and insignificant, if you allude to the motion of a carriage suspended on springs. By observing the degree of heat obtained by different kinds of motion, we may form an estimate of the quantity of exercise given by each. Thus, for example, if you turn out to walk in winter with cold feet, in an hour's time you will be in a glow all over; ride on horseback, the same effect will scarcely be perceived by four hours' round trotting; but if you loll in a carriage, such as you have mentioned, you may travel all day and gladly enter the last inn to warm your feet by a fire. Flatter yourself then no longer that half an hour's airing in your carriage deserves the name of exercise. Providence has appointed few to roll in carriages, while he has given to all a pair of legs, which are machines infinitely more commodious and serviceable. Be grateful, then, and make a proper use of yours. Would you know how they forward the circulation of your fluids in the very action of transporting you from place to place, observe when you walk that all your weight is alternately thrown from one leg to the other; this occasions a great pressure on the vessels of the foot, and repels their contents; when relieved, by the weight being thrown on the other foot, the vessels of the first are allowed to replenish, and by a return of this weight, this repulsion again succeeds; thus accelerating the circulation of the blood. The heat produced in any given time depends on the degree of this acceleration; the fluids are shaken, the humours attenuated, the secretions facilitated, and all goes well; the cheeks are ruddy, and health is established. Behold your fair friend at Auteuil; a lady who received from bounteous nature more really useful science than half a dozen such pretenders to philosophy as you have been able to extract from all your books. When she honours you with a visit, it is on foot. She walks all hours of the day, and leaves indolence, and its concomitant maladies, to be endured by her horses. In this, see at once the preservative of her health and personal charms. But when you go to Auteuil, you must have your carriage, though it is no farther from Passy to Auteuil than from Auteuil to Passy.

Mr. F.

Your reasonings grow very tiresome.

The Gout

I stand corrected. I will be silent and continue my office; take that, and that.

Mr. F.

Oh! Ohh! Talk on, I pray you.

The Gout

No, no; I have a good number of twinges for you

tonight, and you may be sure of some more to-morrow.

Mr. F.

What, with such a fever! I shall go distracted. Oh! eh! Can no one bear it for me?

The Gout

Ask that of your horses; they have served you faithfully.

Mr. F.

How can you so cruelly sport with my torments?

The Gout

Sport! I am very serious. I have here a list of offences against your own health distinctly written, and can justify every stroke inflicted on you.

Mr. F.

Read it then.

The Gout

It is too long a detail; but I will briefly mention some particulars.

Mr. F.

Proceed. I am all attention.

The Gout

Do you remember how often you have promised yourself, the following morning, a walk in the grove of Boulogne, in the garden de La Muette, or in your own garden, and have violated your promise, alleging, at one time, it was too cold, at another too warm, too windy, too moist, or what else you pleased; when in truth it was too nothing but your insuperable love of ease?

Mr. F.

That I confess may have happened occasionally, probably ten times in a year.

The Gout

Your confession is very far short of the truth; the gross amount is one hundred and ninety-nine times.

Mr. F.

Is it possible?

The Gout

So possible that it is fact; you may rely on the accuracy of my statement. You know M. Brillon's gardens, and what fine walks they contain; you know the handsome flight of an hundred steps which lead from the terrace above to the lawn below. You have been in the practice of visiting this amiable family twice a week, after dinner, and it is a maxim of your own, that "a man may take as much exercise in walking a mile up and down stairs, as in ten on level ground." What an opportunity was here for you to have had exercise in both these ways! Did you embrace it, and how often?

Mr. F.

I cannot immediately answer that question.

THE GOUT

I will do it for you; not once.

Mr. F.

Not once?

THE GOUT

Even so. During the summer you went there at six o'clock. You found the charming lady, with her lovely children and friends, eager to walk with you, and entertain you with their agreeable conversation; and what has been your choice? Why, to sit on the terrace, satisfying yourself with the fine prospect, and passing your eye over the beauties of the garden below, without taking one step to descend and walk about in them. On the contrary, you call for tea and the chess-board; and lo! you are occupied in your seat till nine o'clock, and that besides two hours' play after dinner; and then, instead of walking home, which would have bestirred you a little, you step into your carriage. How absurd to suppose that all this carelessness can be reconcilable with health, without my interposition!

Mr. F.

I am convinced now of the justness of Poor Richard's remark, that "Our debts and our sins are always greater than we think for."

42

Dialogue Between The Gout and Mr. F.

THE GOUT

So it is. You philosophers are sages in your maxims, and fools in your conduct.

MR. F.

But do you charge among my crimes that I return in a carriage from M. Brillon's?

THE GOUT

Certainly; for having been seated all the while, you cannot object the fatigue of the day, and cannot want therefore the relief of a carriage.

MR. F.

What then would you have me do with my carriage?

THE GOUT

Burn it if you choose; you would at least get heat out of it once in this way; or if you dislike that proposal, here's another for you; observe the poor peasants who work in the vineyards and grounds about the villages of Passy, Auteuil, Chaillot, etc.; you may find every day among these deserving creatures four or five old men and women, bent and perhaps crippled by weight of years, and too long and too great labour. After a most fatiguing day these people have to trudge a mile or two to their smoky huts. Order your coachman to set them down. This is an act that will be good for your soul; and, at the same time,

43

after your visit to the Brillons, if you return on foot, that will be good for your body.

Mr. F.
Ah! how tiresome you are!

The Gout
Well, then, to my office; it should not be forgotten that I am your physician. There.

Mr. F.
Ohhh! what a devil of a physician!

The Gout
How ungrateful you are to say so! Is it not I who, in the character of your physician, have saved you from the palsy, dropsy, and apoplexy? One or other of which would have done for you long ago but for me.

Mr. F.
I submit, and thank you for the past, but entreat the discontinuance of your visits for the future; for in my mind, one had better die than be cured so dolefully. Permit me just to hint that I have also not been unfriendly to *you.* I never feed physician or quack of any kind, to enter the list against you; if then you do not leave me to my repose, it may be said you are ungrateful too.

The Gout
I can scarcely acknowledge that as any objection. As to quacks, I despise them; they may kill you

indeed, but cannot injure me. And as to regular physicians, they are at last convinced that the gout, in such a subject as you are, is no disease, but a remedy; and wherefore cure a remedy?—but to our business—there.

Mr. F.

Oh! oh!—for Heaven's sake leave me! and I promise faithfully never more to play at chess, but to take exercise daily, and live temperately.

The Gout

I know you too well. You promise fair; but, after a few months of good health, you will return to your old habits; your fine promises will be forgotten like the forms of the last year's clouds. Let us then finish the account, and I will go. But I leave you with an assurance of visiting you again at a proper time and place; for my object is your good, and you are sensible now that I am your *real friend*.

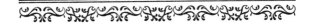

THE WHISTLE

PASSY, NOVEMBER 10, 1779

I RECEIVED my dear Friend's two Letters, one for Wednesday & one for Saturday. This is again Wednesday. I do not deserve one for to-day, because I have not answered the former. But indolent as I am, and averse to Writing, the Fear of having no more of your pleasing Epistles, if I do not contribute to the Correspondance, obliges me to take up my Pen: And as M. Brillon has kindly sent me Word, that he sets out to-morrow to see you; instead of spending this Wednesday Evening as I have long done its Name-sakes, in your delightful Company, I sit down to spend it in thinking of you, in writing to you, & in reading over & over again your Letters.

I am charm'd with your Description of Paradise, & with your Plan of living there. And I approve much of your Conclusion, that in the mean time we should draw all the Good we can from this World. In my Opinion we might all draw more Good, from it than we do, & suffer less Evil, if we would but take care *not to give too much for our Whistles.* For to me it seems that most of the unhappy People we meet with, are become so by Neglect of that Caution.

You ask what I mean? —You love Stories, and will excuse my telling you one of my self. When I was a Child of seven Years old, my Friends on a Holiday fill'd my little Pocket with Halfpence. I went directly to a Shop where they sold Toys for Children; and being charm'd with the Sound of a Whistle that I met by the way, in the hands of another Boy, I voluntarily offer'd and gave all my Money for it. When I came home, whistling all over the House, much pleas'd with my Whistle, but disturbing all the Family, my Brothers, Sisters & Cousins, understanding the Bargain I had made, told me I had given four times as much for it as it was worth, put me in mind what good Things I might have bought with the rest of the Money, & laught at me so much for my Folly that I cry'd with Vexation; and the Reflection gave me more Chagrin than the Whistle gave me Pleasure.

This however was afterwards of use to me, the Impression continuing on my Mind; so that often when I was tempted to buy some unnecessary thing, I said to my self, *Do not give too much for the Whistle*; and I sav'd my Money.

As I grew up, came into the World, and observed the Actions of Men, I thought I met many *who gave too much for the Whistle*. —When

I saw one ambitious of Court Favour, sacrificing his Time in Attendance at Levees, his Repose, his Liberty, his Virtue and perhaps his Friend, to obtain it; I have said to my self, *This Man gives too much for his Whistle.* —When I saw another fond of Popularity, constantly employing himself in political Bustles, neglecting his own Affairs, and ruining them by that Neglect, *He pays*, says I, *too much for his Whistle.* —If I knew a Miser, who gave up every kind of comfortable Living, all the Pleasure of doing Good to others, all the Esteem of his Fellow Citizens, & the Joys of benevolent Friendship, for the sake of Accumulating Wealth, *Poor Man*, says I, *you pay too much for your Whistle.* —When I met with a Man of Pleasure, sacrificing every laudable Improvement of his Mind or of his Fortune, to mere corporeal Satisfactions, & ruining his Health in their Pursuit, *Mistaken Man*, says I, *you are providing Pain for your self instead of Pleasure, you pay too much for your Whistle.* —If I see one fond of Appearance, of fine Cloaths, fine Houses, fine Furniture, fine Equipages, all above his Fortune, for which he contracts Debts, and ends his Career in a Prison; *Alas*, says I, *he has paid too much for his Whistle.* —When I saw a beautiful sweet-temper'd Girl, marry'd to an ill-natured Brute of a Husband; *What a Pity*, says I, *that she should pay so much for a Whistle!* —In short, I conceiv'd that great Part of the Miseries of

Mankind, were brought upon them by the false Estimates they had made of the Value of Things, and by their *giving too much for the Whistle.*

Yet I ought to have Charity for these unhappy People, when I consider that with all this Wisdom of which I am boasting, there are certain things in the world so tempting; for Example the Apples of King John, which happily are not to be bought, for if they were put to sale by Auction, I might very easily be led to ruin my self in the Purchase, and find that I had once more *given too much for the Whistle.*

Adieu, my dearest Friend, and believe me ever yours very sincerely and with unalterable Affection.

THE HANDSOME
AND THE
DEFORMED LEG

THERE are two Sorts of People in the World, who with equal Degrees of Health, & Wealth, and the other Comforts of Life, become, the one happy, and the other miserable. This arises very much from the different Views in which they consider Things, Persons, and Events; and the Effect of those different Views upon their own Minds.

In whatever Situation Men can be plac'd, they may find Conveniencies & Inconveniencies: In whatever Company; they may find Persons & Conversation more or less pleasing. At whatever Table, they may meet with Meats & Drinks of better and worse Taste, Dishes better & worse dress'd: In whatever Climate they will find good and bad Weather: Under whatever Government, they may find good & bad Laws, and good & bad Administration of those Laws. In every Poem or Work of Genius they may see Faults and Beauties. In almost every Face &

every Person, they may discover fine Features & Defects, good & bad Qualities.

Under these Circumstances, the two Sorts of People above mention'd fix their Attention, those who are to be happy, on the Conveniencies of Things, the pleasant Parts of Conversation, the well-dress'd Dishes, the Goodness of the Wines, the fine Weather; &c., and enjoy all with Chearfulness. Those who are to be unhappy, think & speak only of the contraries. Hence they are continually discontented themselves, and by their Remarks sour the Pleasures of Society, offend personally many People, and make themselves everywhere disagreable. If this Turn of Mind was founded in Nature, such unhappy Persons would be the more to be pitied. But as the Disposition to criticise, & be disgusted, is perhaps taken up originally by Imitation, and is unawares grown into a Habit, which tho' at present strong may nevertheless be cured when those who have it are convinc'd of its bad Effects on their Felicity; I hope this little Admonition may be of Service to them, and put them on changing a Habit, which tho' in the Exercise it is chiefly an Act of Imagination yet has serious Consequences in Life, as it brings on real Griefs and Misfortunes. For as many are offended by, & nobody well loves this Sort of People, no one shows them more than the most common civility and respect, and scarcely that;

and this frequently puts them out of humour, and draws them into disputes and contentions. If they aim at obtaining some advantage in rank or fortune, nobody wishes them success, or will stir a step, or speak a word, to favour their pretensions. If they incur public censure or disgrace, no one will defend or excuse, and many join to aggravate their misconduct, and render them completely odious. If these people will not change this bad habit, and condescend to be pleased with what is pleasing, without fretting themselves and others about the contraries, it is good for others to avoid an acquaintance with them; which is always disagreable, and sometimes very inconvenient, especially when one finds one's self entangled in their quarrels.

An old philosophical friend of mine was grown, from experience, very cautious in this particular, and carefully avoided any intimacy with such people. He had, like other philosophers, a thermometer to show him the heat of the weather, and a barometer to mark when it was likely to prove good or bad; but, there being no instrument invented to discover, at first sight, this unpleasing disposition in a person, he for that purpose made use of his legs; one of which was remarkably handsome, the other, by some accident, crooked and deformed. If a Stranger, at the first interview, regarded his ugly Leg more than his handsome one, he doubted him. If he

52

spoke of it, & took no notice of the handsome Leg, that was sufficient to determine my Philosopher to have no further Acquaintance with him. Every body has not this two-legged Instrument, but every one with a little Attention, may observe Signs of that carping, fault-finding Disposition, & take the same Resolution of avoiding the Acquaintance of those infected with it. I therefore advise those critical, querulous, discontented, unhappy People, that if they wish to be respected and belov'd by others, & happy in themselves they should *leave off looking at the ugly Leg*.

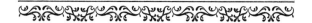

ON WINE

FROM THE ABBÉ FRANKLIN
TO THE ABBÉ MORELLET

You have often enlivened me, my dear friend, by your excellent drinking-songs; in return, I beg to edify you by some Christian, moral, and philosophical reflections upon the same subject.

In vino veritas, says the wise man,—*Truth is in wine*. Before the days of Noah, then, men, having nothing but water to drink, could not discover the truth. Thus they went astray, became abominably wicked, and were justly exterminated by *water*, which they loved to drink.

The good man Noah, seeing that through this pernicious beverage all his contemporaries had perished, took it in aversion; and to quench his thirst God created the vine, and revealed to him the means of converting its fruit into wine. By means of this liquor he discovered numberless important truths; so that ever since his time the word to *divine* has been in common use, signifying originally, *to discover by means of* WINE. (VIN) Thus the patriarch Joseph took upon himself to *divine* by means of a cup or glass of wine, a liquor which obtained this name to show that it was not of human but *divine* invention (another proof of the *antiquity* of the French language, in opposition to M. Gébelin); nay, since that time, all things of peculiar excellence, even the Deities themselves, have been called *Divine* or Di*vin*ities.

We hear of the conversion of water into wine at the marriage in Cana as of a miracle. But this conversion is, through the goodness of God, made every day before our eyes. Behold the rain which descends from heaven upon our vineyards; there it enters the roots of the vines, to be changed into wine; a constant proof that God loves us, and loves to see us happy. The miracle in question was only performed to hasten the operation, under circumstances of present necessity, which required it.

It is true that God has also instructed man to reduce wine into water. But into what sort of water?—*Water of Life.* (*Eau de Vie.*) And this, that man may be able upon occasion to perform the miracle of Cana, and convert common water into that excellent species of wine which we call *punch.* My Christian brother, be kind and benevolent like God, and do not spoil his good drink.

He made wine to gladden the heart of man; do not, therefore when at table you see your neighbor pour wine into his glass, be eager to mingle water with it. Why would you drown *truth*? It is probable that your neighbor knows better than you what suits him. Perhaps he does not like water; perhaps he would only put in a few drops for fashion's sake; perhaps he does not wish any one to observe how little he puts in his glass. Do not, then, offer water, except to children; 't is a mistaken piece of politeness, and often very inconvenient. I give you this hint as a man of the world; and I will finish as I began, like a good Christian, in making a religious observation of high importance, taken from the Holy Scriptures. I mean that the apostle Paul counselled Timothy very seriously to put wine into his water for the sake of his health; but that not one of the apostles or holy fathers ever recommended *putting water to wine*.

P.S. To confirm still more your piety and gratitude to Divine Providence, reflect upon the situation which it has given to the *elbow*. You see (Figures 1 and 2) in animals, who are intended to drink the waters that flow upon the earth, that if they have long legs, they have also a long neck, so that they can get at their drink without kneeling down. But man, who was destined to drink wine, must be able to raise the glass to his mouth. If the elbow had been placed nearer the hand (as in Figure 3), the part in advance would have been too short to bring the glass up to the mouth; and if it had been placed nearer the shoulder, (as in Figure 4) that part would have

Fig. 1.

Fig. 2.

D'après le dessin original envoyé par Franklin .

Fig. 3.

Fig. 4.

Fig. 5.

been so long that it would have carried the wine far beyond the mouth. But by the actual situation, (represented in Figure 5), we are enabled to drink at our ease, the glass going exactly to the mouth. Let us, then, with glass in hand, adore this benevolent wisdom;—let us adore and drink!

BACKGROUND
AND NOTES

BACKGROUND AND NOTES

Bagatelle was a term much in favor in the eighteenth century, when it was fashionable to wrap even the weightiest matters in a cloak of lightheartedness. Having started in Italy as a mountebank's word, meaning a juggler's trick, it soon came to denote, throughout Europe, artistic compositions of an airy, inconsequential nature. Musicians, from Couperin to Beethoven, wrote pieces with that name; when the French King's brother, the Comte d'Artois, built a graceful chateau not far from Franklin's residence at Passy, he called it "Bagatelle."

That Franklin chose to give this title to the literary works he wrote while acting as America's representative at the Court of France does not imply, however, that they were mere trifles: everything he wrote expressed his views, some moral point, some message. Still, in his eyes the Bagatelles were hours of relaxation amid days of hard work and worry, a tribute to feminine charm, a chance to reminisce for an appreciative audience, and a welcome return to the craft of his youth, that of the printer. For the Bagatelles were printed on his own press, in his own house at Passy.

It is easy, in retrospect, to underestimate the hardships he had to overcome during the eight and a half years he lived in France, years now bathed in the glamour of success. When he landed in France in December 1776, the American Revolution was far from won, and all the odds seemed against him. He was seventy years old, afflicted with a stone in the bladder and frequent attacks of gout. His wife had recently died, and his only son, the Royal Governor of New Jersey, had sided with the British and been thrown in jail in Connecticut. He had no staff: his only traveling companions were his seven-year-old grandson, Benny Bache, and William Temple Franklin, the illegitimate son of his illegitimate son, a moody boy of sixteen whose loyalty, at the time, leaned toward his imprisoned father. When Franklin obtained a secretary, it turned out—though he never knew it—that Edward Bancroft was a double agent working slightly more for England's benefit than for America's.

Furthermore, Franklin was a Protestant, coming to ask for aid from a Catholic country. He was a republican, trying to persuade the most conservative continental monarchy to help rebels against another monarchy. He had no well-defined mission: all he had been told by the Committee of Secret Correspondence on the eve of departure was that he should try for anything that could be had, gifts or trade or a full alliance. America, a newcomer as a sovereign state, had no tradition of foreign policy to rely on. His communications with Congress were rare and precarious: in the best of cases it took four to five months for

messages to go back and forth across the Atlantic,
and very often they fell in enemy hands. He received
little support from home: money was scarce, the war
news remained for a long time discouraging. He obtained still less support from his two colleagues on
the American Commission in Paris, Silas Deane who
was embroiled in commercial and financial trouble,
Arthur Lee who quarreled with Deane, with the
French merchants, and with Franklin himself. When
Deane, after a year, was replaced by John Adams, the
latter so antagonized the French Court by his arro-
gance that Foreign Minister Vergennes declared he
would have no further dealings with him. Eventually,
Franklin was rid of both colleagues, which means that
the whole mission fell on his shoulders.

He had to improvise. Diplomatic caution led him
to establish his residence halfway between Paris,
where large crowds were acclaiming him as a hero,
and Versailles, where the Court still was cool and un-
committed. Passy, now one of the most elegant sec-
tions of Paris, was then a charming village; here, in
the wing of the stately Hôtel de Valentinois where he
was living, Franklin could be at the same time aloof
and available. From the depths of his inner being,
from a life richly balanced between private business
and public affairs, scientific research and human so-
ciability, Franklin "the many-faced" now forged the
last of his many personalities, his "French" one.
Happily, his legend corresponded to the sentimental
and intellectual needs of the French. The fashion of
the day called for simplicity and the bucolic ways of
the Trianon; the Philosopher of America dressed
simply and did not wear a wig. People prided them-

selves on their devotion to the sciences; Franklin was the great man of electricity, "l'ambassadeur électrique." The salons of Paris demanded ever new twists of sophistication; Franklin charmed them by his humor and common sense. All this, plus an occasional touch of self-deprecation, explains in part the extraordinary success he obtained in Paris: the Treaty of Amity and Commerce with France, the crucial Treaty of Alliance with France, the recurrent grants of desperately needed money and supplies, and finally the Treaty of Peace with Britain. Not so little, for a man whom John Adams accused of spending a disproportionate amount of time playing chess and drinking tea with the ladies.

Of course, as the Bagatelles attest, Franklin did not deny himself the amusements which French society so bountifully offered him. But he also found time to set up a private press at his home. Shortly after his arrival, he ordered a first batch of type from the Fournier firm, one of the best known in France. Larger quantities followed in 1778 and 1779. In April 1780, he added two printing presses to the equipment he already possessed; his typecasting staff at that time consisted of one foreman and three assistants. When his grandson Benny Bache came back from five years' schooling in Geneva, Franklin installed a master founder at his press to show the boy how to cast type; a few months later, he apprenticed Benny with François Didot, the best printer in France. (Had he not died of the yellow fever in his early thirties, Benny would probably have made his mark in American journalism and printing.)

"Once a printer, always a printer," it has been

said of Franklin; as a matter of fact, the epitaph he chose stresses his pride in having exercised that profession. But the private press at Passy was not merely a hobby. Following his appointment as sole Minister Plenipotentiary (February 1779), Franklin acted singlehandedly as America's Secretary of the Navy, of Commerce, and of Information in Europe. Running one's own press was, under these circumstances, an effective advantage, and even an essential activity. Any printing sent from America was subject to loss or delay, any printing ordered in France entailed the procrastination and prohibitions of government censorship. Only by taking personal care of it could Franklin make sure that an official document issued by him would not be counterfeited. Among such documents printed at the Passy press were passports, blank orders against America's bank balances in France, blank promissory notes and bonds, and regulations concerning the capture of prizes at sea.

In addition, Franklin used his press for his own pursuits, to print the Bagatelles. Because most of them were intended as playful interludes, they probably were not printed in many copies. Now they have become extremely rare, and, some of them, unique. The Mason set at the Yale University Library, here reproduced in facsimile, is the most complete in existence, and contains several unique pieces. We do not know who the original owner was—perhaps Madame Brillon de Jouy, to whom Franklin had sent, by April 1784, "a complete collection of all . . . Bagatelles which have been printed at Passy"—or who, in 1845, had the separate leaflets bound together, apparently at random.

As well as a form of relaxation, the Bagatelles were for Franklin a much needed "exercise in French," and a link between him and the friends who in some cases corrected his style. Never one to praise unduly his senior colleague, John Adams noted: "Dr. F. is reported to speak French very well, but I find upon attending to him critically that he does not speak it grammatically, and indeed upon my asking him sometimes whether a Phrase he had was correct, he acknowledged to me that he was wholly inattentive to the Grammar." As a matter of fact, Franklin found ways to turn his deficiencies to good advantage. "For sixty years, now," he wrote, "masculine and feminine things—and I am not talking about modes and tenses—have been giving me a lot of trouble. I used to hope that at the age of 80 I would be free of all that. But here I am, four times 19, which is mighty close to 80, and those French feminines are still bothering me."

The lady to whom these lines were sent was the one for whom he wrote six of the Bagatelles, Madame Brillon. His neighbor in Passy, she is also, among Franklin's women friends in France, the best known, thanks to the volume and intensity of her correspondence with him, more than one hundred letters. All biographers stress that she was young, lovely, and vibrant. She was all that and more: a distinguished musician, a tormented personality, a possessive and elusive figure frustrated in a marriage to a man twenty-four years her senior, who was rich, jolly, and down-to-earth, but whom she thought culturally inferior. Her relationship with Franklin was complex and ever-changing. It evolved from the conventional flirtation between a prominent statesman and a pretty society woman to the somewhat ambivalent affection of a foster "father" for a tender "daughter" (she called him *papa*); then, after a nervous breakdown on her part, it finally reached a serene plateau.

At some point, Franklin tried to arrange a marriage between his grandson William Temple and the Brillons' older daughter; the proposal was turned down on the grounds of religion and nationality, but the friendship bloomed on. They went on corresponding for the last five years of his life, after Franklin had gone home to Philadelphia and tragedy repeatedly struck the Brillon family. Never forgetting that music had dominated their relations, Franklin, in one of the very last letters he wrote, sent Madame Brillon the words and notes of some recently composed American songs. Most of the Bagatelles written for her are protective and reassuring, as if Franklin were trying to encourage her, to shield her as much from the turmoils of her own spirit as from the shocks of the outside world.

Three of the other pieces have a more pronounced didactic undertone. Two of them, "Information to Those Who Would Remove to America" and "Remarks on the Politeness of the Savages of North America," were meant to give the general public a better idea of the reality of American life. Especially in the "Information," one catches glimpses of the self-righteous side of Franklin's character that so irritated critics like Mark Twain and D. H. Lawrence. But the two pieces, though included in the Bagatelles, are parts of the earnest message the American Minister Plenipotentiary wanted to convey, blending a measure of propaganda with a goodly amount of straightforward information, and seasoning it with wit. Another message, which had also appeared in one of the Bagatelles written for Madame Brillon, is entrusted to the "Parable Against Persecution." Its theme, religious toleration, had long been dear to Franklin, and found a most appreciative audience in the "enlightened" circles of France. As to the "Letter to the Royal Academy," it is the only example in the Bagatelles of a broader type of humor, which Franklin did not print without some misgivings, for it "has too much *grossièreté* to be borne by the polite readers of this nation."

A spirit of urbane exuberance and conviviality pervades the remaining four Bagatelles, to which has been added the "Letter on Wine," not included by Franklin in his printed collection. They were meant for the group that became known as "L'Académie d'Auteuil"—the wits and thinkers who belonged to the Masonic Lodge of the philosopher Claude-Adrien Helvétius and flocked to his widow's new residence near the Bois de Boulogne after his death.

Franklin professed a measure of spiritual kinship with the late Helvétius. Yet his homespun philosophy was much more moderate than *De l'Esprit*, which stressed personal interest as the basic human motivation, and was condemned by the Parliament of Paris. (Stendhal himself, who, much later, called Helvétius' book a milestone of the eighteenth century, regretted that the philosopher had not written "pleasure" instead of "interest.") Nevertheless, Franklin sought for admission to the Lodge of the Nine Sisters in 1777 and was chosen its Grand Master (*Vénérable*) the following year. But he attended still more often, and with greater pleasure, the informal meetings at Madame Helvétius' home.

A beautiful woman in her youth, she was in her sixties when Franklin met her—a mercurial, independent, unconventional personality, aristocratic by birth, bohemian by temperament. It was said that she loved every living creature, except women. Her entourage liked to tease her about the number of cats, dogs, birds, deer, and other animals she surrounded herself with, but she merely laughed and acquired some more. Very responsive to her robust *joie de vivre*, Franklin wanted to marry her and remain in France for the rest of his life. She said no, but kept his devotion, as she had kept that of the great economist Turgot, another rejected but affectionate suitor.

When Franklin left for America, in July 1785, Madame Helvétius, in a rare outburst of emotion, tried to call him back: "I cannot get accustomed to the idea that you have left us . . . that I shall never see you again. I can picture you in your litter, further from us at every step, already lost to me and to your friends who loved you so much and regret you so. I fear you are in pain. . . . If such is the case, come back, my dear friend, come back to us. You will make our life happier. . . ."

But he was on his way. Still, she was the only one to whom he wrote from Le Havre: "We shall stay here a few days, waiting for our luggage, and then we shall leave France, the country that *I love the most* in the world. And there I shall leave my dear Helvetia. She may be happy yet. I am not sure that I shall be happy in America, but I must go back. I feel sometimes that things are badly arranged in this world when I consider that people so well matched to be together are forced to separate. I will not tell you of my love. . . . I only hope that you will always love me some. Think of me sometimes and write sometimes to your

Benjamin Franklin"

CLAUDE-ANNE LOPEZ, Assistant Editor
The Papers of Benjamin Franklin, Yale University

Remarks on the Politeness
of the Savages of North America

THROUGHOUT his career Franklin was a defender of mistreated minorities—including women—and wrote both pleas for justice and satires on their behalf. An early example is "The Speech of Polly Baker," wherein a spirited young woman, brought to court for having five illegitimate children, turns on her judges, describes the cowardice of the men who took advantage of her, and defends her way of life. Franklin's last public act was a petition to Congress in 1789 attacking slavery, signed by him as President of the Abolition Society.

Thus even in his early years his advocacy of moderation was accompanied by an active defense of the freedom of the individual and his right to live according to unconventional standards. Here he employs an objective appreciation of the merits of Indian manners to expose the hypocrisy of white men, playing the part of iconoclast with a forensic wit not unrelated to that of Voltaire.

Bilked for Breakfast

IN QUICK, simple French, this sketch introduces the whole lively Helvétius household. Living in good-humored informality as permanent guests were two abbés—André Morellet, a well-known economist, then in his fifties, Martin Lefebvre de la Roche, some years younger, a librarian and connoisseur of fine books—and a young doctor, Pierre-Georges Cabanis, who was to make a name for himself in the field of medicine and political theory. A frequent and always welcome visitor to Auteuil, Franklin gloried in a variety of friendships with the members of the "family," including Madame's married daughters and her grandchildren. These he called the stars and the little stars, whereas for the hostess he coined the title of "Notre Dame d'Auteuil."

Little is known about the Madame La Freté to whom the mock lament was sent (her husband had business dealings with the colonies). She was one of the many women with whom Franklin corresponded in the gallant manner of the day.

Years later, back in Philadelphia, he evoked with longing the atmosphere of Auteuil: "Yesterday was a Wednesday. At ten in the Morning, I thought of you, of your House, your Table, your Friends. At this Hour, said I to myself, all of them are dining . . . the Abbés de la Roche and Morellet, M. Cabbanis, perhaps some of the little Stars. Madame serves the whole Company, with as much ease as pleasure. But, alas, I was not there to take my share in the lovely, sensible talk...."

The Flies

WHEREAS the letter to Madame La Freté depicts Madame Helvétius as something less than a well-organized hostess, "The Flies" show that she was capable of domestic concern on Franklin's behalf.

His apartments were a separate wing on a fine estate, the Hôtel de Valentinois, overlooking the Seine. He maintained a warm relationship with his landlord, Jacques-Donatien Leray de Chaumont, an enterprising man of wealth, as well as with Madame de Chaumont and their children (one of whom emigrated to the United States, where he built, in Chaumont, New York, a small replica of the Hôtel de Valentinois).

The eloquent flies are one more instance of Franklin's pleasure in the device of lending human voices to animals and objects. It has been suggested that the flies' idle life was meant to symbolize the parasitic existence of the French courtiers. But it seems unlikely that Franklin would have featured a class he had no respect for to convey a message that was close to his heart. He certainly wished to merge his ménage with that of Madame Helvétius.

The Elysian Fields

FRANKLIN'S intentions in writing and then publishing this Bagatelle are appropriately mysterious and may never be fully known. It is most probable, though not absolutely certain, that he actually did propose to Madame Helvétius. He could have meant his letter as a half serious request for reconsideration, a face-saving hint that he had spoken in jest, or even as a *jeu d'esprit*. Comments range from that of Sainte-Beuve, who felt "one can sense a deep emotion underlying the playful surface," to that of Abbé Morellet, who stated that Madame Helvétius received the Bagatelle "one morning, after spending the previous day talking a lot of nonsense with Franklin."

Long a member of the household, Morellet was accustomed to being teased on account of his voracious appetite for cream: nor, it is known, did bibliophile Abbé de la Roche resent the fact that Madame Helvétius paid so little heed to his suggestions.

In order to become fully accepted in that intimate circle, Franklin, too, soon resigned himself to a rebuke said to stem from Madame's determination to remain faithful to the memory of her husband, a philosopher Franklin admired. In turn, Madame Helvétius did not mind being jokingly told by a mutual friend after Franklin's return to America, that his "absence and love" were the cause of a "fit of weakness" she suffered. "She does not blush," the friend reported, "but only answers, friendship and true regrets hurt full as much."

Parable Against Persecution

To FRANKLIN no subject was too sacred for a hoax, including the Bible. He once proposed a new version of the English Bible that would make it more fashionably "modern" and therefore more generally acceptable. As a sample he "modernized" part of the first Chapter of the Book of Job, which began: "Verse 6. And it being *levée* day in heaven, all God's nobility came to court, to present themselves before him: and Satan also appeared in the circle, as one of the ministry." On another occasion, he rewrote the Lord's Prayer, as an exercise in precise meaning.

The "Parable Against Persecution" apparently satisfied a wish to add a Chapter to the Old Testament in keeping with his ideas of religious tolerance. It is said that he took considerable pleasure in inserting it as if it belonged to the text while reading the Bible out loud to friends.

———

*To The Royal Academy of * * * * **

IN THE original manuscript the asterisks are replaced by the word "Brussels." A few years before, the Académie Royale des Sciences des Lettres et des Beaux-Arts de Belgique, at Brussels, is on record as having instituted a study to investigate a possible relation between meteorology and public sanitation.

Franklin had short patience with academic pomposity, and a strong liking for puns, which were much in style at the time.

In 1783 he wrote a friend in England that "All the conversation here at present turns upon the Balloons filled with light inflammable air. . . . Inflammable air puts me in mind of a little jocular paper I wrote some years since in ridicule of a prize Question given out by a certain Academy on this side the Water, and I enclose it for your amusement."

A further example of his interest in "hot air" is to

be found in a hoax he wrote as an anonymous letter to a Paris newspaper, signed by a "lady correspondent," about efforts to discover a new air to lift balloons. In it he said: "If you want to fill your balloons with an element ten times lighter than inflammable air, you can find a great quantity of it, and ready made, in the promises of lovers and of courtiers and in the sighs of widowers; in the good resolutions taken during a storm at sea, or on land, during an illness; and especially in the praise to be found in letters of recommendation."

———

A Tale

Though the pointed allusions to denominational exclusivism in "A Tale" applied more particularly to the rival churches in America, the warm plea for religious toleration struck a most responsive chord in the land of Voltaire. It is worth noting that, in his original manuscript, Franklin had been still kinder to the non-sectarian good man than in the printed version: poor Montrésor was told by St. Peter to take a place not merely "wherever you can," but "wherever you wish."

The Bagatelle has a parallel in a letter Madame Brillon wrote to Franklin. "When I go to Paradise," she said, "if St. Peter asks me of what religion I am, I shall answer him: 'Of the religion whereby people love all those who resemble him. I have loved and idolized Doctor Franklin.' I am sure that St. Peter will say: 'Come in and go promptly to take place next to Mr. Franklin. You shall find him seated next to the Eternal Being.' "

The shortest of Franklin's Bagatelles was nevertheless the one which won the broadest acclaim: by the turn of the century, the story had been republished no less than five times, with and without modifications.

———

Information to Those
Who Would Remove to America

THIS vision of America (the only piece in the collection that is not really a Bagatelle), written in 1784, reflects both Franklin's nostalgia on his eighth year away from home and the general tenor of much of the mail he received, which included an avalanche of tedious requests. As he wrote on March 9, 1784, to Charles Thomson, President of Congress: "I am pestered continually with Numbers of Letters from People in different Parts of Europe, who would go to settle in America, but who manifest very extravagant Expectations, such as I can by no means encourage; and who appear otherwise to be very improper Persons. To save myself Trouble I have just printed some Copies of the enclosed little Piece, which I purpose to send hereafter in Answer to such Letters."

Here, Franklin, the journalist, no longer the diplomat, drops for once his attitude of benevolence toward all things French. Through the biting remarks of a Negro slave, he reveals some of his revulsion towards the economic injustices and the social iniquities of the *ancien régime*.

━━━━

The Ephemera

THIS celebrated Bagatelle is a token of Franklin's admiration for Madame Brillon, whose name is easily recognized under the "aimable Brilliante" of the last line. In the second summer of their friendship (1778), she sometimes took him to Moulin-Joly, an "English" (that is, informal) garden on a little island in the Seine, which belonged to the painter Claude-Henri Watelet. "At the Time when the Letter was written," Franklin explained later to a friend, "all conversations in Paris were filled with Disputes about the Musick of Gluck and Picciny, a German and an Italian Musician, who divided the Town into Violent Parties." Queen Marie-Antoinette was on Gluck's side, and posterity tends to agree with her, but most of the Passy group held for Piccini. On this and other occasions, Franklin, a rather taciturn man, was taken aback by Gallic loquacity. "If you French would only talk four at a time," he is reported to have said, "one might understand you."

"The thought," he wrote, "was partly taken from a Little Piece of some unknown Writer which I met with 50 Years since in a Newspaper, and which the Sight of the Ephemera brought to my Recollection." As a matter of fact, he had reprinted the little piece in his own *Pennsylvania Gazette* for December 4, 1735.

The Moulin-Joly did not survive the "old grey-headed Ephemera" by very long: it was dismantled during the French Revolution.

———

The Philosopher and The Gout and Dialogue Between The Gout and Mr. Franklin

IN THE fall of 1780, Franklin was afflicted with a severe attack of the gout. Madame Brillon, on the verge of what was to be a major illness, was having one of her frequent nervous upsets, and had to stay home, too. The two friends, denied for months their bi-weekly meetings, resorted to correspondence, with Monsieur Brillon acting as messenger.

In a rare moment of high spirits, Madame Brillon wrote "Le Sage et La Goutte," a little fable in verse in the style of La Fontaine, in which she adopted toward Franklin's disease the usual attitude of good-humored chiding. Gout, it was believed, was the by-product of gastronomic and amorous excesses. Franklin replied: "One of the characters of your Fable, Madame La Goutte, seems to me to reason pretty well, except when she supposes that Mistresses have had a share in producing this painful Malady. I, for one, believe the exact opposite; and here is my argument. When I was a young man and enjoyed more of the favors of the sex than I do at present, I had no Gout. *Hence*, if the ladies of Passy had shown more of that Christian charity that I have so often recommended to you in vain, I should not be suffering from the Gout right now."

A while later, stimulated by Madame Brillon's poem, Franklin wrote his "Dialogue," in French, had it revised by a friend and sent it to her for additional comments. The manuscript, with Madame Brillon's annotations in the margin, still exists. She protested that whoever had corrected his text had blundered, that his own French, though unorthodox, was more pungent, more original.

The list of place names mentioned by The Gout refers to the homes of ladies Franklin frequently visited. Passy, of course, is Madame Brillon, and Auteuil is Madame Helvétius. Montmartre is the peppery Madame Le Roy, whom Franklin called his "little pocket-wife." She was married to his colleague in physics, Jean-Baptiste Le Roy. Sanoy is the famous Countess d'Houdetot, Rousseau's former flame, who gave a much noted "philosophical feast" in the Doctor's honor.

Franklin acknowledged Madame Brillon as the source of his initial inspiration. When he sent her a set of the printed Bagatelles he wrote: "I beg your pardon for having put among those of my own, one of your creation, which is certainly too charming to be placed in such Company." Her fable is the only piece not written by Franklin himself to have been printed and included in his collection.

The Whistle

ALWAYS high-strung, Madame Brillon was very badly shaken upon discovering that her husband had been having an affair with their children's governess.

In her distress, she turned for comfort, more than
ever, to a Franklin now firmly cast in the role of
father. From her mother's estate, where she was
visiting, she sent him dispirited messages on every
one of *their* Wednesdays and Saturdays, the days
when she and Franklin would regularly meet when
she was in residence at Passy, "that sacred little portion of the week," as Franklin put it.

In one letter, as a counterpoise to all that was dis-
tressing her in real life, she painted her idea of Paradise: no more partings, a diet of roasted apples, Scot-
tish tunes (Franklin's favorites), chess games all
ending in a tie, a single language for all, no jealousy,
no amorous dalliance, no gout, no nerves. . . . To
these romantic longings Franklin countered with his
"Story of the Whistle," a level-headed formula for
enjoying life such as it is: keep a sense of proportion.
But Madame Brillon, in her answer, only reflected
despondently that, by putting her trust in the wrong
people, she had indeed paid a high price for some
very bad whistles.

The allusion to King John's apples—one of several
in Franklin's letters—must have hinted to some private joke between them.

The Handsome and the Deformed Leg

FRANKLIN was so pleased by Madame Brillon's fa-
vorable reaction to his "Dialogue" that within a
month he was working on what was to become another
Bagatelle. On November 23, 1780, he wrote to her:

"Since you show some Partiality toward my little Writings, I am sending you a Piece that I wrote in English during my illness. It may afford you a Moment's Amusement. The Translation is by Mr. Cabbanis. I think you make fun of me when you say that my poor French is better before being corrected than afterwards. . . ."

Franklin does not mention the title of this "new little writing." But Madame Brillon's answer, two days later, gives a clue: "Between the two of us, my good friend, we would not make two instruments equipped with good and bad legs, for I fear that our four legs are not worth a single mediocre one." The story thus alluded to can only be "The Handsome and Deformed Leg," a summing up of Franklin's outlook on life, of his belief that, in spite of circumstances, we make ourselves into what we want. His eye was not on the best of all *conceivable* worlds but on the best of all *possible* worlds. Such a world, he now tried to tell Madame Brillon, could be attained by her.

———

On Wine

THE LETTER on Wine sent to Abbé Morellet has the character of a Bagatelle, though Franklin did not print it on his private press. With its cascade of partly untranslatable puns (*vin*, wine; *deviner*, to guess at, to soothsay; *divin*, divine; *eau-de-vie*, water of life, that is aquavit, brandy, etc.), it belongs to the kind of message inspired by an intimate, convivial friendship.

Background and Notes

The exchange which led to the letter probably began when Abbé Morellet composed a poem purporting to reveal the hidden causes of the American Revolution: the English were forcing the Americans to drink tea or, at best, muddy wine, whereas the aim of the colonies was to drink claret or French champagne. Quickly replying in kind, Franklin sent a drinking song *he* had written in his youth. It was a dialogue between the Singer, who suggests various ways to happiness (love, wealth, power) and the Chorus who invariably answers:

> O No!
> Not so!
> For honest Souls know
> Friends and a Bottle will bear the Bell.

Soon after, Franklin followed his song with the letter on Wine, which includes a reference to the theory of a primitive, universal language espoused by their common friend Court de Gébelin in his *Monde Primitif*. The illustrations accompanying the letter were drawn by one of Franklin's grandsons.

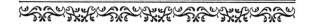

THE TEXT
AND THE FACSIMILE

T H E Bagatelles were originally printed as separate leaflets and pamphlets, some in French, some in English and French. "The Ephemera" and the "Parable Against Persecution," printed only in French by the Passy press, exist in English in manuscript in Franklin's own hand, and the manuscripts have been used to provide the English text in this edition. For the other Bagatelles printed only in French by Franklin, the English versions, after diligent comparisons, have been selected by and revised by Mr. Willard R. Trask. In each case, the earliest traditional yet faithful translation has been chosen, except in the case of three of the Bagatelles, which Mr. Trask translated anew for this edition: "Bilked for Breakfast," "The Flies," and "A Tale." (For further information concerning translations, consult the Bibliography.)

"The Philosopher and The Gout," the fable in verse by Madame Brillon, was translated by Irene Orgel.

"The Handsome and The Deformed Leg," while not included in the "Mason Copy" volume here reproduced in facsimile, was printed by the Passy press in French and has survived. It is larger in format than the others, and printed in double columns on the face of a single sheet. "The Morals of Chess" is mentioned in a letter from Franklin to Madame Brillon as being one of the Bagatelles from Passy, but a printed copy has never been found; the text has not been included here. "Information to Those Who Would Remove to America," the longest of the Bagatelles, appears in the facsimile in both English and French. Because of its utilitarian nature and its difference from the others, a modern setting of it has not been provided.

The order of presentation of the translations of the Bagatelles in this edition has been chosen by the publishers in terms of a unity of interest for the contemporary reader rather than on a strict historical or chronological basis. "Remarks on the Politeness of the Savages of North America" is placed first because it is impersonal and clearly modern in outlook, as well as a fine introductory example of Franklin's ability to combine seriousness and humor. The three Bagatelles after are concerned with Madame Helvétius and life at Auteuil, the four next following are addressed to a more general public, and the last six (except for the final one) are addressed to Madame Brillon. "On Wine," was not issued by the Passy press, but was later printed in the "Mémoires inédits" of the Abbé Morellet, with the accompanying drawings.

The facsimile portion of this book includes two versions of "The Elysian Fields" which differ from each other slightly.

The famous and unique bound copy of the Bagatelles in the William Smith Mason Collection at Yale University is reproduced here in its entirety.

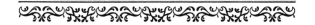

A LITERARY NOTE

I<small>T</small> IS known that Franz Kafka read and admired Benjamin Franklin. The attraction is understandable. Different as they were, Kafka and Franklin both sought through the exercise of the imagination to consecrate life. Each consolidated his own creative image of man; each saw human society as an allegory, a vision.

They were masters of opposites, the one of frustration, the other of fulfillment. Whereas the intellections of Kafka were crystalized from the insights of a prophetic fatalism, Franklin was a fatalist of hope. His prayer was action, to give life grace, and his form of grace was *invention*.

D. H. Lawrence, another temperament, found Franklin a worthy adversary. But it was the side of Franklin that sought through maxims and homilies to survive and surmount the labyrinth of responsible action which Lawrence took literally and could not abide. The older Franklin, who fell in love with Paris was—we find in Franklin's Bagatelles—perhaps as free and physical a soul as Lawrence.

Franklin loved women. He was not sentimental about youth, age, or health. His freedom was that of the eighteenth century; it lived in the masque of formality. To a vital contemporary of Mozart and Casanova (and of Figaro and Don Juan), sex was a civilized passion, courtship an art, and "sublimation" itself a delight in social intercourse.

A Literary Note

His superb intelligence, especially in the Bagatelles, is a tonic antidote to twentieth-century barbarities, the treadmill of Freudianisms, and sham sociologies claiming to be culture. It is perhaps characteristic of conventionality and philistinism in each age to reduce complexity to cliché. A complex genius, Franklin toughly believed in *toleration* of the different, and *courtesy* of behavior, as preconditions of an *effective* radical revolution in culture—the democratic revolution. (Observers as profound as Stendhal soon after despaired of democracy, foreseeing the momentum of vulgarity, the romanticism of violence, the cheap thrill becoming almost totally ascendant, as in our own day.)

Influenced by Addison and Fielding, Rabelais and Swift, throughout his life Franklin wrote and published literary jokes and moral tracts. In France, nearing the end of his life, the moral gift was transformed into the Bagatelle, the point becoming an earthy felicity touched with the élan of bliss.

The Bagatelles deserve to be read as literature. The voice that speaks to us through them is perennially modern, rediscovered each generation. Such a mind reaches across time, showing the seed of *virtu* in the blossom of human foible, tossing the lie of a gallant muse into the teeth of death and vice.

Leslie Katz

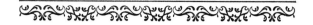

SELECTED BIBLIOGRAPHY

Franklin and his French Contemporaries
  Alfred Owen Aldridge
  New York, New York University Press, 1957

Franklin's Wit and Folly
  Richard E. Amacher
  New Brunswick, New Jersey, Rutgers
  University Press, 1953

Franklin and his Press at Passy
  Luther S. Livingston
  New York, The Grolier Club, 1914

Mon Cher Papa: Franklin and the Ladies of Paris
  Claude-Anne Lopez
  New Haven, Yale University Press, 1966

Benjamin Franklin
  Carl Van Doren
  New York, The Viking Press, 1938

Benjamin Franklin's Autobiographical Writings
  Selected and edited by Carl Van Doren
  New York, The Viking Press, 1945

The Papers of Benjamin Franklin
  Sponsored by the American Philosophical
  Society and Yale University
  Edited by Leonard W. Labaree
  New Haven, Yale University Press, 1959

Selected Bibliography

"Franklin and his Press at Passy" (An Article)
F. B. Adams, Jr.
Yale University Library Gazette, XXX,
No. 4, April, 1956

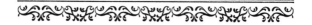

ACKNOWLEDGEMENTS

SPECIAL thanks are due the Yale University Library for permission to reproduce the copy of Franklin's *Bagatelles* in the William Smith Mason Collection. We wish to express our appreciation to Mr. Archibald Hanna, Jr., Curator of the Benjamin Franklin Collection at Yale, for his cooperation and interest. We wish to thank also Leonard W. Labaree, Farnam Professor Emeritus of History and Editor of *The Papers of Benjamin Franklin*.

Claude-Anne Lopez, the author of *Mon Cher Papa* and Assistant Editor of *The Papers of Benjamin Franklin*, in addition to writing the Background and Notes, made valuable suggestions, and was generous of her time and efforts on behalf of this edition.

Mr. Willard R. Trask, the translator, also contributed helpful editorial advice.

The drawing of the Hôtel Valentinois is reproduced with the kind permission of the Grolier Club, from *Franklin and his Press at Passy*, by Luther S. Livingston.

The endpapers are from a cotton panel, entitled "The Apotheosis of Franklin," made in England c. 1790, reproduced courtesy of the Cooper Union Museum, New York, New York.

THE PUBLISHERS

BAGATELLES.

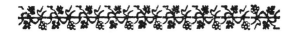

DIALOGUE

ENTRE

LA GOUTTE ET M. F.

à Minuit le 22 Octobre 1780.

M. F.

EH ! oh ! eh ! Mon Dieu ! qu'ai-je fait pour mériter ces souffrances cruelles ?

LA GOUTTE.

Beaucoup de choses. Vous avez trop mangé, trop bu , & trop indulgé vos jambes en leur indolence.

M. F.

Qui est-ce qui me parle ?

LA GOUTTE.

C'est moi-même , la goutte.

M. F.

Mon ennemie en personne !

LA GOUTTE.

Pas votre ennemie.

A ij

M. F.

Oui , mon ennemie ; car non - feulement vous voulez me tuer le corps par vos tourmens , mais vous tâchez auffi de détruire ma bonne réputation. Vous me repréfentez comme un gourmand & un ivrogne. Et tout le monde qui me connoît , fçait qu'on ne m'a jamais accufé auparavant d'être un homme qui mangeoit trop , ou qui buvoit trop.

La Goutte.

Le monde peut juger comme il lui plaît. Il a toujours beaucoup de complaifance pour lui-même , & quelquefois pour fes amis. Mais je fçais bien , moi , que ce qui n'eft pas trop boire , ni trop manger pour un homme qui fait raifonnablement d'exercice , eft trop pour un homme qui n'en fait point.

M. F.

Je prends , — eh ! eh ! — autant d'exercice, — eh ! — que je puis , Madame la Goutte. Vous connoiffez mon état fédentaire , & il me femble , qu'en conféquence vous pourriez, Madame la Goutte , m'épargner un peu, confidérant que ce n'eft pas tout-à-fait ma faute.

La Goutte.

Point du tout. Votre Rhétorique & votre Politeffe font également perdues. Votre ex-

eufe ne vaut rien. Si votre état eft fédentaire,
vos amufemens, vos recreations doivent être
actifs. Vous devez vous promener à pied ou
à cheval ; ou fi le temps vous en empêche,
jouer au billard. Mais examinons votre cours
de vie. Quand les matinées font longues &
que vous avez affez de temps pour vous promener, qu'eft-ce que vous faites ? Au lieu de
gagner de l'appetit pour votre déjeuner par
un exereice falutaire, vous vous amufez à
lire des livres, des brochures, ou gazettes
dont la plupart n'en valent pas la peine. Vous
déjeunez néanmoins largement ; quatre taffes
de thé à la crême avec une ou deux tartines
de pain & de beurre couvertes de tranches de
bœuf fumé, qui, je crois, ne font pas les
chofes du monde les plus faciles à digérer.
Tout de fuite vous vous placez à votre bu-
reau, vous y écrivez, ou vous parlez aux
gens qui viennent vous chercher pour affaire.
Cela dure jufqu'à une heure après midi fans
le moindre exercice de corps. Mais tout cela
je vous le pardonne, parce que cela tient,
comme vous dites, à votre *état fédentaire*.
Mais après dîner, que faites-vous ? Au lieu
de vous promener dans les beaux jardins de
vos amis chez lefquels vous avez dîné, comme
font les gens fenfés, vous voilà établi à l'échiquier jouant aux échecs, où on peut vous
trouver deux ou trois heures. C'eft-là votre
recréation éternelle ! La recréation qui de

A iij

toutes eſt la moins propre à un homme ſéden-
taire ; parce qu'au lieu d'accélérer le mouvement des fluides , il demande une attention ſi
forte & ſi fixe , que la circulation eſt retardée
& les ſecrétions internes empêchées. Enve-
loppé dans les ſpéculations de ce miſérable
jeu, vous détruiſez votre conſtitution. Que
peut-on attendre d'une telle façon de vivre
ſinon un corps plein d'humeurs ſtagnantes
prêtes à ſe corrompre , un corps prêt à tomber
en toutes ſortes de maladies dangereuſes , ſi
moi , la Goute , je ne viens pas de temps en
temps à votre ſecours pour agiter ces humeurs,
& les purifier ou diſſiper ? Si c'étoit dans
quelque petite rue ou coin de Paris , dépourvu
de promenades , que vous paſſiez quelque
temps aux échecs après dîner , vous pourriez
dire cela en excuſe : mais c'eſt la même choſe
à Paſſy , à Auteuil , à Montmartre, à Epinay,
à Sanoy où il y a les plus beaux jardins &
promenades & belles Dames, l'air le plus pur,
les converſations les plus agréables , les plus
inſtructives , que vous pouvez avoir tout en
vous promenant , mais tous ſont négligés
pour cet abominable jeu d'échecs. Fi donc ,
M. F. ! Mais en continuant mes inſtructions ,
j'oubliois de vous donner vos corrections.
Tenez cet élancement ; & celui ,

M. F.

Oh ! eh ! oh ! ohhh ! — Autant que vous

voudrez de vos inftructions , Madame la Goutte , même de vos reproches , mais de grace plus de vos corrections.

LA GOUTTE

Tout au contraire , je ne vous rabattrois pas le quart d'une. Elles font pour votre bien. Tenez.

M. F.

Oh ! ehhh ! — Ce n'eft pas jufte de dire que je ne prends aucun exercice. J'en fais fou - vent dans ma voiture, en fortant pour aller à dîner , & en revenant.

LA GOUTTE.

C'eft de tous les exercices imaginables le plus léger & le plus infignifiant que celui qui eft donné par le mouvement d'une voiture fufpendue fur des refforts. En obfervant la quantité de chaleur obtenue de différentes ef- peces de mouvement , on peut former quelque jugement de la quantité d'exercice qui eft donnee par chacun. Si , par exemple , vous fortez à pied en hiver , avec les pieds froids , en marchant une heure , vous aurez vos pieds & tout votre corps bien échauffés. Si vous montez à cheval , il faut troter quatre heures avant de trouver le même effet ; mais fi vous vous placez dans une telle voiture , vous pou- vez voyager toute une journée , & entrer

A iv

votre derniere auberge avec vos pieds encore
froids. — Ne vous flattez donc pas qu'en paſ-
ſant une demi-heure dans votre voiture vous
preniez de l'exercice. Dieu n'a pas donné des
voitures à roues à tout le monde , mais il a
donné à chacun deux jambes, qui ſont des
machines infiniment plus commodes & plus
ſerviables ; ſoyez-en reconnoiſſant , & faites
uſage des vôtres. Voulez vous ſavoir comment
elles font circuler vos fluides en même temps
qu'elles vous tranſportent d'un lieu à un autre , penſez que quand vous marchez , tout le
poids de votre corps eſt jetté alternativement
ſur l'une & l'autre jambe ; cela preſſe avec
grande force ſur les vaiſſeaux du pied , & re-
foule ce qu'ils contiennent. Pendant que le
poids eſt ôté de ce pied & jetté ſur l'autre ,
les vaiſſeaux ont le temps de ſe remplir, &
par le retour du poids , ce refoulement eſt
répété, ainſi la circulation du ſang eſt accélérée
en marchant. La chaleur produite en un certain
eſpace de temps eſt en raiſon de l'accélération ;
les fluides ſont battus , les humeurs atténuées ,
les ſecrétions facilitées , & tout va bien. Les
joues prennent du vermeil , & la ſanté eſt
établie. Regardez votre amie d'Auteuil , une
femme qui a reçu de la nature plus de ſcience
vraiment utile , qu'une demi-douzaine enſem-
ble de vous Philoſophes prétendus n'en n'ont
tiré de tous vos livres. Quand elle voulut
vous faire l'honneur de ſa viſite , elle vint à

pied; elle fe promene du matin jufqu'au foir, & elle laiffe toutes les maladies d'indolence en partage à fes chevaux. Voilà comme elle conferve fa fanté, même fa beauté. Mais vous, quand vous allez à Auteuil c'eft dans la voiture. Cependant il n'y a pas plus loin de Paffy à Auteuil, que d'Auteuil à Paffy.

M. F.

Vous m'ennuiez avec tant de raifonnemens.

LA GOUTTE.

Je le crois bien. Je me tais, & je continue mon office. Tenez cet élancement, & celui-ci.

M. F.

Oh ! ohh ! — Continuez de parler, je vous prie.

LA GOUTTE.

Non. J'ai un nombre d'élancemens à vous donner cette nuit, & vous aurez le refte demain.

M. F.

Mon Dieu, la fievre! Je me perds. Eh ! eh ! N'y a-t-il perfonne qui puiffe prendre cette peine pour moi.

LA GOUTTE.

Demandez cela à vos chevaux. Ils ont pris la peine de marcher pour vous.

A v

M. F.

Comment pouvez-vous être si cruelle, de me tourmenter tant pour rien.

L A G O U T T E.

Pas pour rien. J'ai ici une liste de tous vos péchés contre votre santé, distinctement écrite, & je peux vous rendre raison de tous les coups que je vous donne.

M. F.

Lisez-la donc.

L A G O U T T E.

C'est trop long à lire. Je vous en donnerai le montant.

M. F.

Faites-le. Je suis tout attention.

L A G O U T T E.

Souvenez-vous combien de fois vous vous êtes proposé de vous promener le matin suivant dans le bois de Boulogne, dans le jardin de la Muette ou dans le vôtre ; & que vous avez manqué de parole ; alleguant quelquefois que le temps étoit trop froid, d'autrefois qu'il étoit trop chaud, trop venteux, trop humide, ou trop quelqu'autre chose, quand en verité, il n'y avoit rien de trop qui empêchoit, excepté votre trop de paresse.

M. F.

Je confesse que cela peut arriver quelque-fois, peut-être pendant un an dix fois.

LA GOUTTE.

Votre confession est bien imparfaite, le vrai montant est cent quatre-vingt-dix-neuf.

M. F.

Est-il possible !

LA GOUTTE.

Oui; c'est possible, parce que c'est un fait. Vous pouvez rester assuré de la justesse de mon compte. — Vous connoissez les jardins de M. B****, comme ils sont bons à pro-mener. Vous connoissez le bel escalier de cent cinquante degrés qui méne de la terrasse en haut, jusqu'à la plaine en bas. Vous avez visité deux fois par semaine dans les après midi cette aimable famille ; c'est une maxime de votre invention, qu'on peut avoir autant d'exercice en montant & en descendant un mille en escalier, qu'en marchant dix sur une plaine. Quelle belle occasion vous avez eue de prendre tous les deux exercices ensemble. En avez-vous profité ? & combien de fois ?

M. F.

Je ne peux pas bien répondre à cette question.

L A G O U T T E.

Je répondrai donc pour vous. Pas une fois.

M. F.

Pas une fois !

L A G O U T T E.

Pas une fois. Pendant tout le bel été passé vous y êtes arrivé à six heures. Vous y avez trouvé cette charmante femme & ses beaux enfans , & ses amis , prêts à vous accompagner dans ces promenades , & de vous amuser avec leurs agréables conversations. Et qu'avez-vous fait ? Vous vous êtes assis sur la terrasse , vous avez loué la belle vue , regardé la beauté des jardins en bas ; mais vous n'avez pas bougé un pas pour descendre vous y promener. Au contraire vous avez demandé du thé & l'échiquier. Et vous voilà collé à votre siége jusqu'à neuf heures. Et cela après avoir joué peut-être deux heures où vous avez dîné. Alors, au lieu de retourner chez vous à pied, ce qui pourroit vous remuer un peu , vous prenez votre voiture. Quelle sottise de croire qu'avec tout ce déréglement , on peut se conserver en santé sans moi.

M. F.

A cette heure je suis convaincu de la justesse de cette remarque du bon homme Richard, que nos dettes & nos péchés font toujours plus grands qu'on ne pense.

LA GOUTTE.

C'eſt comme cela, que vous autres Philoſophes avez toujours les maximes des Sages dans votre bouche, pendant que votre conduite eſt comme celle des ignorans.

M. F.

Mais faites-vous un de mes crimes de ce que je retourne en voiture chez Me. B****?

LA GOUTTE.

Oui aſſûrement ; car vous qui avez été aſſis toute la journée, vous ne pouvez pas dire que vous êtes fatigué du travail du jour. Vous n'avez pas beſoin donc d'être ſoulagé par une voiture.

M. F.

Que voulez-vous donc que je faſſe de ma voiture ?

LA GOULTE.

Brûlez-la, ſi vous voulez. Alors vous en tirerez au moins pour une fois de la chaleur. Ou ſi cette propoſition ne vous plaît pas, je vous en donnerai une autre. Regardez les pauvres payſans qui travaillent la terre dans les vignes & les champs autour des villages de Paſſy, Auteuil, Chaillot, &c. vous pouvez

tous les jours , parmi ces bonnes créatures ,
trouver quatre ou cinq vieilles femmes &
vieux hommes , courbés & peut-être eſtropiés
ſous le poids des années & par un travail trop
fort & continuel , qui , après une longue
journée de fatigue , ont à marcher peut-être
un ou deux milles pour trouver leurs chau-
mieres. Ordonnez à vorre cocher de les prendre & de les placer chez eux. Voilà une bonne
œuvre ! qui ſera du bien à votre ame ; & ſi
en même temps vous retournez de votre viſite
chez les B * * * * à pied , cela ſera bon pour
votre corps.

M. F.

Ah ! comme vous êtes ennuyeuſe !

L A G O U T T E.

Allons donc à notre métier , il faut ſouve-
nir que je ſuis votre Médecin. Tenez.

M. F.

Ohhh ! —Quel diable de Médecin !

L A G O U T T E.

Vous êtes un ingrat de me dire cela. N'eſt-
ce pas moi qui , en qualité de votre Médecin,
vous ai ſauvé de la paralyſie , de l'hydropiſie
& de l'apoplexie , dont l'une ou l'autre vous
auroient tué il y a long-temps , ſi je ne les en
avois empêchée.

M. F.

Je le confeſſe. Et je vous remercie pour ce qui eſt paſſé. Mais de grace quittez-moi pour jamais. Car il me ſemble qu'on aimeroit mieux mourir que d'être guéri ſi douloureuſement. Souvenez-vous que j'ai auſſi été votre ami. Je n'ai jamais loué de combattre contre vous, ni les Médecins, ni les Charlatans d'aucune eſpece ; ſi donc vous ne me quittez pas , vous ſerez auſſi accuſable d'ingratitude.

LA GOUTTE.

Je ne penſe pas que je vous doive grande obligation de cela. Je me moque des Charlatans ; ils peuvent vous tuer , mais ils ne peuvent pas me nuire. Et quant aux vrais Médecins , ils ſont enfin convaincu de cette vérité , que la goutte n'eſt pas une maladie, mais un véritable rémede ; & qu'il ne faut pas guérir un remede. Revenons à notre affaire. Tenez.

M. F.

Oh de grace quittez-moi, & je vous promets fidélement que déſormais je ne jouerai plus aux échecs , que je ferai de l'exercice journellement , & que je vivrai ſobrement.

LA GOUTTE.

Je vous connois bien : vous êtes un beau prometteur ; mais après quelques mois de bonne santé, vous commencerez à aller votre ancien train. Vos belles promesses seront oubliées comme on oublie les formes des nuages de la derniere année. Allons donc, finissons notre compte. Après cela je vous quitterai ; mais soyez assuré que je vous revisiterai en temps & lieu : car c'est pour votre bien , & je suis, vous sçavez , votre bonne amie.

A V I S

A CEUX

QUI VOUDRAIENT S'EN ALLER

EN AMERIQUE.

———

M, DCC, LXXXIV.

A V I S

A CEUX

QUI VOUDRAIENT S'EN ALLER EN AMERIQUE.

PLUSIEURS Perſonnes en Europe ayant té-
moigné directement ou par Lettres à l'Auteur de cet
Ecrit, qui connoît très-bien l'Amérique Septentrionale, le Déſir d'y paſſer & de s'y établir ; comme
il lui paroît que, par Ignorance, ils ont pris des
Idées & des Eſpérances fauſſes ſur ce qu'ils pour-
roient y obtenir, il croit faire une choſe utile, &
qu'il épargnera des Inconvéniens des Voyages & des
Déplacemens coûteux & ſans Fruit, aux Perſonnes
à qui ce Parti ne convient pas, en donnant ſur cette
Région quelques Notions plus claires & plus ſures que
celles qui ont prévalu juſqu'à préſent.

Il voit que pluſieurs imaginent que les Habitans
de l'Amérique Septentrionale ſont riches, en état
& dans la Diſpoſition de récompenſer toute Eſpece
d'Induſtrie ; qu'en même temps ils ignorent toutes
les Sciences, & conſéquemment que les Etrangers
qui poſſédent des Talens dans les *Belles-Lettres* &

A 2

les beaux Arts doivent y être grandement eſtimés, & ſi bien payés qu'ils deviendront aiſément riches ; qu'il y a auſſi grand Nombre d'Offices avantageux dont on peut diſpoſer, & qui demandent pour les remplir des Qualités que les Naturels n'ont pas ; & que, comme parmi eux il y a peu de Gens de Famille , les Etrangers de Naiſſance doivent y être fort reſpectés, & par conſéquent faire tous Fortune en obtenant facilement les meilleurs de ces Offices ; que le Gouvernement auſſi , pour encourager les Emigrations d'Europe, non ſeulement paye la Dépenſe du Tranſport perſonnel , mais donne gratis aux Etrangers des Terres avec des Négres pour les cultiver, des Outils de Labourage & des Beſtiaux; ce ſont de pures Imaginations , & ceux qui vont en Amérique avec des Eſpérances fondées ſur ces Idées ſe trouveront certainement trés-loin de Compte.

Quoiqu'il y ait, à la Vérité, dans ce Pays peu d'Hommes auſſi miſérables que les Pauvres d'Europe, il y a en auſſi très-peu de ceux qu'on y appelle riches ; il y regne plutôt une heureuſe & générale Médiocrité ; il y a peu de grands Propriétaires de Terre & peu de Tenanciers. La plus grande Partie des Hommes cultive ſes propres Champs, les autres s'attachent à quelque Métier ou Négoce ; fort peu ſont aſſez riches pour vivre ſans rien faire, ſur leur Revenus , ou pour payer les hauts Prix qu'on donne en Europe pour les Peintures , les Sculptures, les Ouvrages d'Architecture & autres Produits de l'Art qui ſont plus curieux qu'utiles ; delà ceux qui ſont nés en Amérique avec des Diſpoſitions naturelles pour ces Talens, ont, ſans Exception, quitté ce Pays pour l'Europe, où ils peuvent être plus avantageuſement récompenſés. Il eſt vrai que les Lettres & les Connoiſſances mathématiques y ſont en Eſtime, mais elles ſont en même

temps plus communes qu'on ne le croit, puisqu'il
exiſte déja neuf Colléges ou Univerſités, ſavoir :
quatre dans la Nouvelle-Angleterre & une dans
chacun des Etats de New-York, New-Jerſey,
Penſilvanie, Maryland & Virginie, toutes pour-
vues de ſavans Profeſſeurs, ſans compter nombre
d'Académies moins conſidérables ; elles enſeignent
à une Partie de leur Jeuneſſe les Langues & les
Sciences néceſſaires à ceux qui ſe deſtinent à être
Prêtres, Avocats ou Médecins. On n'emploie certainement aucuns Moyens pour exclure les Etrangers
de ces Profeſſions ; & le prompt Accroiſſement d'Habitans par tout peut leur procurer l'Avantage d'être
employés comme les Naturels du Pays. Il n'y a
qu'un petit Nombre d'Offices civils ou d'Emplois ;
il n'y en a point de ſuperflus, comme en Europe ;
la Regle établie dans quelques Etats eſt, qu'aucun
Office ne doit être aſſez lucratif pour être déſirable.
Le 36 Article de la Conſtitution de Penſilvanie s'ex-
prime préciſément en ces Mots : *Comme pour con-
ſerver ſon Indépendance, tout Homme libre, (s'il
n'a pas un Bien ſuffiſant,) doit avoir quelque
Profeſſion ou quelque Métier, faire quelque Commerce, ou tenir quelque Ferme qui puiſſent le faire
ſubſiſter honnêtement, il ne peut y avoir ni Né-
ceſſité, ni Utilité d'établir des Emplois lucratifs,
dont les Effets ordinaires ſont dans ceux qui les
poſſédent ou qui les recherchent, une Dépendance
ou une Servitude indignes d'Hommes libres ; &
dans le Peuple, des Querelles, des Factions, la
Corruption & le Déſordre ; c'eſt pourquoi toutes
les fois que par l'Augmentation de ſes Émolumens,
ou par quelque autre Cauſe, un Emploi deviendra
aſſez lucratif pour émouvoir le Deſir & attirer la
Demande de pluſieurs Perſonnes, le Corps légiſ-
latif aura Soin d'en diminuer les Profits.*

A 3

Ces Idées étant plus ou moins fortement établies
dans tous les Etats-Unis, il ne peut être raisonna-
ble pour aucun Homme, ayant des Moyens de vivre
chez lui, de s'expatrier dans l'Espoir d'obtenir en
Amérique un Office civil avantageux ; & les Emplois militaires sont finis avec la Guerre, puisqu'on
a licentié l'Armée. Il est beaucoup moins sensé
d'y aller n'ayant d'autre Titre de Recommandation
que sa Naissance ; elle a sans Doute sa Valeur en
Europe ; mais c'est une Denrée qu'on ne peut pas
porter à un plus mauvais Marché qu'à celui de l'A-
mérique, où on ne demande point à l'Egard d'un
Etranger, *qui est-il ?* mais, *que sait-il faire ?*
S'il possede quelque Art utile, il est le Bien-venu ;
s'il l'exerce & qu'il se conduise bien, il sera res-
pecté par tous ceux qui le connoîtront ; mais celui
qui n'est pas autre Chose qu'un Homme de Qualité,
qui, pour cette Raison, veut vivre aux Dépens du
Public par quelqu'Office ou Salaire, sera regardé
de mauvais œil & méprisé. Le Laboureur y est en
Honneur, & même l'Ouvrier, parce que leurs Occupations sont utiles ; le Peuple a Coutume de dire
que Dieu tout-puissant est lui-même un Artisan, le
plus habile qui soit dans l'Univers, & ils le respec-
tent & l'admirent plus pour la Variété, l'Industrie
& l'Utilité de ses Ouvrages qu'à cause de l'Anti-
qnité de sa Famille. Ils aiment l'Observation d'un
Négre, & ils la répétent souvent dans son mauvais
Anglois : que Boccarorra (c'est à dire l'Homme blanc)
fait travailler un Noir, fait travailler un Cheval,
fait travailler un Bœuf, fait travailler tout le
Monde, excepté le Cochon ; il ne peut pas faire
travailler le Cochon ; il mange, il boit, il se promene, il va dormir quand il lui plaît, il vit comme
un Gentilhomme. D'après ces Opinions des Amé-
ricains, ils se croiroient beaucoup plus obligés à

un Généalogiste qui leur prouverait que leurs Ancê-
tres & leurs Alliés ont été pendant dix Générations,
Laboureurs, Forgerons, Charpentiers, Tourneurs,
Tisserands, Tanneurs ou même Cordonniers, & par
conféquent des Membres utiles de la Société, que,
s'il ne pouvoit que leur prouver qu'ils ont été Gen-
tilhommes, ne se souciant que de vivre, sans rien
faire, du Travail des autres, vraiment *fruges consumere nati* *, & d'ailleurs bons à rien, jusqu'à ce
qu'après leur Mort on puisse dépecer leur Fortune
comme la Personne du Cochon Gentilhomme du
Négre.

À l'Egard des Encouragemens de la Part du Gouvernement pour les Etrangers, il n'y a réellement
que ceux qui dérivent des bonnes Loix & de la
Liberté ; ils y sont bien reçus, parce qu'il y a suffi-
samment Place pour tous, & que conféquemment
les anciens Habitans n'en sont point jaloux. Les
Loix les défendent assez pour qu'ils n'aient pas
besoin de la Protection d'un Grand, & chacun jouit
avec Sécurité des Profits de son Savoir-faire ; mais
s'il n'a pas apporté de Fortune il faut qu'il travaille
pour vivre, & qu'il soit industrieux. Un ou deux
Ans de Résidence lui donnent tous les Droits de
Citoyen ; mais quoiqu'ait pu faire autrefois le Gouvernement, il ne forme à présent de Convention
avec personne pour l'engager à s'établir, soit en
payant son Passage, soit en lui donnant des Terres,
des Négres, des Outils, des Troupeaux, ou aucune
Espece d'Emolument ; enfin l'Amérique est le
Pays de Travail, & nullement ce que les Anglais
appellent *Lubberland*, & les Français, *Pays de*

---

* *Nos numeri sumus fruges consumere nati.*
HOR.

A 4

Cocagne, où les Rues font, dit-on, pavées de petits Pains, les Maifons couvertes d'Omelettes, & où les Poulardes voltigent, toutes roties, en criant: *Venez me manger.*

A quelle Efpece d'Hommes donc ferait-il aujourd'hui profitable de fe tranfportèr en Amérique ? & quels Avantages pourraient-ils raifonnablement attendre ?

Le Pays eft rempli d'immenfes Forêts vuides d'Habitans , & qui ne feront pas occupées d'un Siécle ; & la Terre eft à fi bon marché, que la Propriété de cent Acres d'un Sol fertile , couvert de Bois, peut s'acquérir, dans beaucoup d'Endroits près des Frontieres, pour huit ou dix Guinées. De jeunes Laboureurs vigoureux, qui s'entendent à la Culture des Grains & au Soin des Beftiaux, qui font à-peu-près les mêmes là qu'en Europe, peuvent facilement s'y établir. Un peu d'Argent mis à part fur les gros Gages qu'ils y reçoivent lorfqu'ils travaillent pour les autres, les met en état d'acheter un Terrein, & de commencer leur Plantation, ils font aidés par la bonne Volonté de leurs Voifins & quelque Crédit. Une Multitude de pauvre Peuple d'Angleterre , d'Irlande, d'Ecoffe & d'Allemagne font en peu d'Années devenus, par ces Moyens, de riches Cultivateurs, tandis que dans leur Pays, où les Terres font toutes occupées, & le Prix du Travail modique, ils n'auraient jamais pu fe tirer de la chétive Condition dans laquelle ils étoient nés.

La Bonté de l'Air, la Salubrité du Climat, l'Abondance de Nourritures faines, & l'Encouragement à fe marier de bonne heure par la Certitude d'avoir une Subfiftance en cultivant la Terre, font que l'Accroiffement des Habitans par la feule Fécondité du Pays eft très-rapide, & devient encore plus confidérable par l'Addition des Etrangers. Il en réfulte

qu'on a toujours befoin d'un grand Nombre d'Artifans pour tout ce qui eſt néceſſaire & utile, pour
garnir les Ménages des Cultivateurs & leur fournir
les Outils de la forte la plus groſſiere, & qu'il feroit
plus incommode d'apporter d'Europe. Dans tous
les Métiers de cette Eſpece, les Ouvriers paſſable-
ment bons font furs de trouver de l'Emploi & d'être
bien payés de leurs Ouvrages; il n'y a aucune En-
trave qui puiſſe gêner les Étrangers dans l'Exercice
du Métier qu'ils favent, & ils n'ont pas befoin de
Permiſſion; s'ils font pauvres, ils commencent par
être Domeſtiques ou Journaliers, & s'ils font fobres,
intelligens & ménagers, ils deviennent bientôt
Maîtres, ils travaillent pour leur propre Compte,
fe marient, élevent leur Famille & deviennent des
Citoyens reſpectables.

Auſſi ceux qui n'ayant qu'une Fortune médiocre
& pluſieurs Enfans à pourvoir, fouhaitent leur donner de l'Induſtrie & aſſurer du Bien à leur Poſtérité,
ont ils la Facilité de faire à cet Egard en Amérique
ce qui leur ferait impoſſible en Europe. Ils peuvent, fans craindre d'être mépriſés, apprendre &
pratiquer des Arts méchaniques lucratifs, ils feront
au contraire reſpectés s'ils deviennent habiles. Les
petits Capitaux employés à l'Achat des Terres, qui
journellement augmentent de Valeur par l'Accroiſ-
fement de la Population, donnent la Perſpective
d'une ample Fortune dans la Suite pour les Enfans.
L'Auteur de cet Ecrit a vu pluſieurs Exemples de
grands Terreins, fur les Frontieres qu'avoit alors la
Penſilvanie, achetés dix livres Sterlings les cent
Acres, qui vingt Ans après, lorſque les Habitations
fe font étendues beaucoup audelà, fe vendaient cou-
ramment, fans qu'on y eut fait aucune Amélioration,
trois livres Sterling par Acre; l'Acre d'Amérique eſt
le même qu'en Angleterre & en Normandie.

117

Ceux qui veulent fe mettre au Fait de l'Etat du
Gouvernement feront bien de lire les Conftitutions
des différens Etats & les Articles de la Confédération qui les lie tous enfemble pour les Affaires géné-
rales fous la Direction d'une Affemblée qu'on appelle Congrès. Ces Conftitutions ont été impri-
mées en Amérique par fon Ordre ; on en a fait deux
Editions à Londres, & on en a publié dernierement
à Paris une bonne Traduction Françaife.

Ces dernieres Années plufieurs Souverains d'Europe ont cru qu'il leur ferait avautageux de faire
fabriquer dans leurs propres Etats ce qui fert aux
Commodités de la Vie, d'établir des Manufactures
pour diminuer & rendre nulles les Importations, &
ils ont entrepris d'attirer les Fabricans des autres
Pays par de hauts Salaires, des Priviléges, &c.
Plufieurs Perfonnes prétendant fe bien connaître dans
différentes Sortes de Manufactures en grand, ont
imaginé que l'Amérique devait en avoir befoin, que
le Congrès feroit probablement dans la Difpofition
des Souverains dont nous venons de parler, & ont
propofé de s'y tranfporter à Condition qu'on paye-
rait leur Paffage, qu'on leur donneroit des Terres,
des Salaires, des Privileges exclufifs pour plufieurs
Années, &c., ces Perfonnes en lifant les Articles
de la Confédération, trouveront que le Congres n'a
ni Pouvoir pour cet Objet, ni Argent entre fes
Mains pour de femblables Projets, & qu'il n'y auroit que le Gouvernement de quelqu'Etat particulier qui put donner un pareil Encouragement : on
l'a toutefois rarement accordé en Amérique ; &
quand on l'a fait, on n'a prefque jamais réuffi à
établir des Manufactures que le Pays, encore trop
faible, ne pouvait pas encourager les Particuliers
à monter eux-mêmes. Le Travail eft généralement
trop cher & les Travailleurs trop difficiles à confer-

ver, chacun defirant d'être Maître ; & le bon Marche
des Terres donnant à beaucoup le Defir de quitter
les Métiers pour l'Agriculture. Quelques-unes, à
la Vérité, ont été établies & conduites avec Succès ;
mais ce font en général celles qui ne demandent que
peu de Bras, & dans lefquelles la plus grande Partie
des Ouvrages fe font par des Machines. Les Mar-
chandifes trop volumineufes & d'une fi petite Valeur qu'elles ne peuvent pas fupporter la Dépenfe
du Fret, peuvent fouvent être fabriquées à meilleur
Marché dans les Pays que celles qu'on pourrait im-
porter, & les Manufactures de ces Objets feront
avantageufes par-tout où il y aura fuffifamment de
demandes. Les Agriculteurs, à la Vérité, récol-
tent en Amérique beaucoup de Laine & de Lin,
& on n'en exporte point, tout eft mis en œuvre,
mais dans des Atteliers domeftiques pour l'Ufage de
la Maifon. On a plufieurs fois entrepris dans différens Etats, d'en acheter une grande Quantité
pour les faire filer, employer des Tifferands & former des grands Etabliffemens qui fabriquaffent de
la Toile & des Ouvrages de Laine pour les vendre ;
mais ces Projets ont prefque toujours mal tourné,
parce qu'on importe des Ouvrages auffi bons & à
meilleur compte ; & lorfque les Gouvernemens ont
été follicités pour foutenir & encourager ces Etabliffemens par de l'Argent, ou en impofant des
Droits fur l'Importation des Objets de même Efpece,
ils l'ont toujours refufé, fur le Principe, que fi la
Province eft affez floriffante pour avoir des Manufactures, les Particuliers peuvent en établir avec
Profit ; & que, dans le Cas contraire, c'eft une
Folie de vouloir forcer la Nature. Les Manufactures en grand demandent beaucoup de Pauvres qui
travaillent pour un léger Salaire : on peut les trouver en Europe ; mais il n'y en aura point en Amé-

rique jufqu'à ce que les Terres foient toutes prifes
& cultivées, & que ceux qui ne pourront én avoir
aient befoin d'être employés. Les Manufactures de
Soie, dit-on, font naturelles en France, comme
celles de Draps en Angleterre, parce que chacun
de ces Pays produit en Abondance la Matiere pre-
miere; mais fi l'Angleterre veut avoir des Manufactures de Soie, comme celles de Laine, & la France
des Manufactures de Laine, comme celles de Soie,
il faut que ces Opérations forcées foient foutenues,
comme on l'a fait effectivement, par des Prohibitions mutuelles, ou de forts Droits fur l'un & l'autre Marchandife importée. Par ce Moyen les Ouvriers peuvent forcer ceux qui les confomment fur
le Lieu, d'en donner un plus haut Prix, fans que
cette Augmentation les rende plus heureux, ou plus
riches; il arrive feulement qu'ils en boivent davan-
tage & travaillent moins. Les Gouvernemens en
Amérique ne donnent donc aucun Encouragement à
de pareilles Entreprifes; &, par ce Moyen, on n'y
eft point rançonné par les Marchands, ou par les
Ouvriers. S'il arrive qu'un Marchand demande trop
pour des Souliers importés, on les achette chez un
Cordonnier, & fi celui-ci veut un Prix trop fort,
on les prend chez le Marchand; de cette Maniere
ces deux Etats font contenus l'un par l'autre:
tout Calcul fait cependant, le Cordonnier en Amérique peut retirer de fon Ouvrage un Profit plus
confidérable qu'en Europe; car il peut ajouter au
Prix qu'on y donne une Somme à-peu-prés égale à
la Dépenfe du Fret, de la Commiffion, des Rifques
ou de l'Affurance, &c. que fupporte néceffairement
le Marchand; & il en eft de même pour les Ouvriers
de tout autre Art méchanique; en Conféquence les
Artifans en général vivent mieux & plus aifément
en Amérique qu'en Europe, & ceux qui font Eco-

nomes mettent à part une bonne Réferve pour le
Soutien de leur Vieilleffe & de leurs Enfans ; il peut
donc être avantageux pour cette Efpece d'Hommes
de paffer en Amérique.

Dans les Contrées d'Europe habitées depuis long-
temps, les Arts, les Métiers, les Profeffions, les
Fermages, &c. font tous tellement remplis qu'il eft
difficile pour les Gens pauvres de placer leurs Enfans de Maniere qu'ils puiffent gagner, ou apprendre à gagner de quoi vivre d'une Maniere fupporta-
ble. Les Artifans qui craignent de fe donner pour
l'Avenir des Rivaux dans leur Métier, ne prennent
point d'Apprentifs, à moins qu'on ne leur donne de
l'Argent & de quoi les entretenir, ou l'Equivalent,
ce que les Parens ne font pas en Etat de faire ; il
s'en fuit que les jeunes Gens ignorent, fans pouvoir
faire autrement, toute Efpece d'Art lucratif, &
deviennent par Néceffité Soldats, Domeftiques ou
Voleurs pour fubfifter. En Amérique l'Accroiffement rapide des Habitans écarte la Crainte de cette
Rivalité ; les Artifans reçoivent volontiers des Apprentifs dans l'Efpoir de retirer le Profit de leur
Travail pendant le Refte du Temps ftipulé par de-là
celui néceffaire pour qu'ils foient formés ; il n'eft
par conféquent pas difficile aux Familles pauvres de
faire inftruire leurs Enfans, & les Artifans font
tellement empreffés d'avoir des Eléves, que plufieurs d'entr'eux donneront même de l'Argent aux
Pere & Mere pour s'attacher leurs Garçons de dix à
quinze Ans jufqu'à celui de vingt & un, & par ce
Moyen plufieurs pauvres Parens, à leur Arrivée
dans le Pays, ont eu de quoi acheter des Terres
fuffifamment pour s'établir, & faire fubfifter le
Refte de leur Famille par l'Agriculture. Ces Con-
ventions pour les Apprentifs font faites devant un
Magiftrat, qui en regle les Conditions fuivant la

Raiſon & la Juſtice; & dans la Vue de former pour l'Avenir un utile Citoyen, il oblige le Maître de s'engager par un Contrat écrit, non-ſeulement à ce que pendant le Temps du Travail ſtipulé l'Apprentif ſoit convenablement nourri, déſaltéré, vêtu, blanchi & logé, mais à lui donner à l'Expiration de ſon Temps un Aſſortiment complet de Vêtemens neufs, qu'en outre on lui montrera à lire, à écrire & à compter, & qu'il ſera bien inſtruit dans l'Art ou la Profeſſion de ſon Maître, ou dans quelqu'autre qui le mette en Etat par la Suite de gagner de quoi vivre & d'élever à ſon tour une Famille. On donne une Copie de cette Convention à l'Eléve, ou à ceux qui s'intéreſſent à lui; le Magiſtrat l'écrit ſur un Régiſtre, & on peut y avoir Recours ſi le Maître manque en aucun Point de l'exécuter. Ce Déſir qu'ont les Maîtres d'avoir un plus grand Nombre de Bras pour leurs Ouvrages les engage à payer le Paſſage des jeunes Gens de l'un & de l'autre Sexe qui conſentent à leur Arrivée de les ſervir un, deux, trois ou quatre Ans. Ceux qui ſavent déja faire quelque Choſe obtiennent un Terme plus court, à Raiſon de leur Adreſſe, & un Prix juſtement proportionné à leur Service; ceux qui ne ſavent rien, s'engagent pour un plus long Terme, afin qu'on leur montre un Metier que leur Pauvreté ne leur a pas permis d'apprendre dans leur Pays.

La Médiocrité qui regne preſque généralement en Amérique dans les Fortunes, obligeant ſes Habitans à faire quelque choſe pour ſubſiſter, prévient en grande Partie les Vices qui naiſſent ordinairement de la Fainéantiſe; l'Induſtrie jointe à une Occupation conſtante eſt un grand Préſervatif pour les Mœurs & la Vertu d'une Nation; il arrive de-là que la Jeuneſſe a plus rarement en Amérique de mauvais Exemples, ce qui doit être une Conſidéra-

tion bien fatisfaifante pour des Parens. On peut
encore certainement ajouter à ces Avantages que
non feulement on y tolere la Religion fous fes
différentes Dénominations, mais même qu'on l'y
refpecte & la cultive; l'Athéïfme y eft inconnu,
l'Incrédulité rare & fécrette, deforte qu'on peut y
vivre long-temps fans être fcandalifé par le Rencontre d'un Athée ou d'un Incrédule ; & la Divi-
nité paroît avoir montré manifeftement qu'elle approuve la Tolérance & la Douceur avec lefquelles
les différentes Sectes fe traitent l'une l'autre, par
la grande Profpérité dont elle a bien voulu favorifer
tout le Pays.

A Paſſy, le 10 Novembre 1779.

J'AI reçu les deux Lettres de ma chere Amie, l'une pour le Mercredi, l'autre pour le Samedi. C'eſt aujourd'hui encore Mercredi. Je ne mérite pas d'en avoir encore, parce que je n'ai pas fait Réponſe aux précédentes. Mais tout indolent que je ſuis, & quelque Averſion que j'aie d'écrire, la Crainte de n'avoir plus de vos charmantes Epitres, ſi je ne contribue auſſi ma part pour ſoutenir la Correſpondance, me force de prendre la Plume. Et comme M. B. m'a mandé ſi obligeamment qu'il part demain matin pour vous voir, moi, au lieu de paſſer ce Mercredi au ſoir, comme je l'ai fait ſi long-temps de ſes Prédéceſſeurs du même Nom, en votre douce Société, je me ſuis mis à mon Ecritoire pour le paſſer à penſer à vous, à vous écrire, & à lire & relire ce que vous m'avez ſi délicieuſement écrit.

Je ſuis charmé de votre Deſcription du Paradis, & de vos Plans pour y vivre. J'approuve auſſi très-fortement la Concluſion que vous faites, qu'en attendant il faut tirer de ce bas Monde tout le Bien qu'on en peut tirer. A mon Avis il eſt très-poſſible pour nous d'en tirer beaucoup plus de Bien, que nous n'en tirons, & d'en ſouffrir moins de mal, ſi nous voulions ſeulement prendre garde de ne donner pas trop pour nos Sifflets. Car il me ſemble que la plupart des Malheureux qu'on trouve dans le Monde, ſont devenus tels par leur Négligence de cette Précaution.

Vous demandez ce que je veux dire ? — Vous aimez les Hiſtoires, & vous m'excuſerez ſi je vous en donne qui me regarde moi-même. Quand

I RECEIVED my dear Friend's two Letters, one for Wedneſday & one for Saturday. This is again Wedneſday. I do not deſerve one for to day, becauſe I have not anſwered the former. But indoſent as I am, and averſe to Writing, the Fear of having no more of your pleaſing Epiſtles, if I do not contribute to the Correſpondance, obliges me to take up my Pen : And as M. B. has kindly ſent me Word, that he ſets out to-morrow to ſee you ; inſtead of ſpending this Wedneſday Evening as I have long done its Name-ſakes , in your deſightful Company, I ſit down to ſpend it in thinking of you, in writing to you, & in reading over & over again your Letters.

I am charm'd with your Deſcription of Paradiſe, & with your Plan of living there. And I approve much of your Concluſion, that in the mean time we ſhould draw all the Good we can from this World. In my Qpinion we might all draw more Good, from it than we do , & ſuffer leſs Evil, if we would but take care *not to give too much for our Whiſtles.* For to me it ſeems that moſt of the unhappy People we meet with, are become ſo by Neglect of that Caution.

You ask what I mean? ― You love Stories , and will excuſe my telling you one of my ſelf. When I was a Child of ſeven Years old, my Friends on a Holiday fill'd my little Pocket with Halfpence. I went directly to a Shop where they ſold Toys for Children ; and being charm'd with the Sound of a Whiſtle that I met by the way, in the hands of another Boy, I voluntarily offer'd and gave all my Mo-

j'étois un Enfant de cinq ou six ans, mes Amis, un Jour de Fête, remplirent ma petite Poche de Sols. J'allai tout de suite à une Boutique où on vendoit des Babioles ; mais étant charmé du Son d'un Sifflet que je rencontrai en Chemin dans les mains d'un autre petit Garçon, je lui offris & donnai volontiers pour cela tout mon Argent. Revenu chez moi, sifflant par toute la Maison, fort content de mon Achat, mais fatiguant les Oreilles de toute la Famille, mes Freres, mes Sœurs, mes Cousines, entendant que j'avois tant donné pour ce mauvais Bruit, me dirent que c'étoit dix fois plus que la Valeur ; alors ils me firent penser au Nombre de bonnes Choses, que je pouvois ache-ter avec le Reste de ma Monnoie, si j'avois été plus prudent, & ils me ridiculiserent tant de ma Follie, que je pleurois de cette Vexation ; & la Réflexion me donnoit plus de Chagrin, que le Sifflet de Plaisir.

Cet Accident fut cependant dans la Suite de quel-que Utilité pour moi, l'Impression restant sur mo[n] Ame ; de sorte que, lorsque j'étois tenté d'achet.r quelque Chose qui ne m'étoit pas nécessaire, je disois en moi-même, Ne donnons pas trop pour le Sifflet : & j'épargnois mon Argent.

Devenant grand Garçon, entrant dans le Monde & observant les Actions des Hommes, je vis que je rencontrois Nombre de Gens qui donnoient trop pour le Sifflet.

Quand j'ai vu quelqu'un, qui, ambitieux de la Faveur de la Cour, consumoit son Temps en Assiduités aux Levers, son Repos, sa Liberté, sa Vertu, & peut-être ses vrais Amis, pour obtenir quelque petite Distinction ; j'ai dis en moi-même, Cet Homme donne trop pour son Sifflet. — Quand j'en ai vu une autre, avide de se rendre populaire, & pour cela s'occupant toujours de Contestations

ney for it. When I came home, whistling all over the
House, much pleas'd with my Whistle, but disturbing
all the Family, my Brothers, Sisters & Cousins,
understanding the Bargain I had made, told me I
had given four times as much for it as it was worth,
put me in mind what good Things I might have
bought with the rest of the Money, & laught at
me so much for my Folly that I cry'd with Vexation; and the Reflection gave me more Chagrin
than the Whistle gave me Pleasure.

This however was afterwards of use to me, the
Impression continuing on my Mind; so that often
when I was tempted to buy some unnecessary thing,
I said to my self, *Do not give too much for the
Whistle;* and I sav'd my Money.

As I grew up, came into the World, and observed the Actions of Men, I thought I met many
who gave too much for the Whistle. --When I saw
one ambitious of Court Favour, sacrificing his
Time in Attendance at Levees, his Repose, his
Liberty, his Virtue and perhaps his Friend, to
obtain it; I have said to my self, *This Man gives
too much for his Whistle.* --When I saw another
fond of Popularity, constantly employing himself
in political Bustles, neglecting his own Affairs,
and ruining them by that Neglect, *He pays,* says I,
too much for his Whistle. --If I knew a Miser,
who gave up every kind of comfortable Living,
all the Pleasure of doing Good to others, all the
Esteem of his Fellow Citizens, & the Joys of benevolent Friendship, for the sake of Accumulating
Wealth, *Poor Man,* says I, *you pay too much
for your Whistle.* --When I met with a Man of
Pleasure, sacrificing every laudable Improvement
of his Mind or of his Fortune, to mere corporeal
Satisfactions, & ruining his Health in their Pursuit,
Mistaken Man, says I, *you are providing Pain*

publiques , négligeant fes *Affaires* particulieres,
& les ruinant par cette Négligence ; Il paye trop,
ai-je dit , pour fon Sifflet. -- *Si j'ai connu un
Avare* , qui renonçoit à toute Maniere de vivre
commodement , à tout le Plaifir de faire le bien aux
autres , à toute l'Eftime de fes Compatriotes , &
à tous les Charmes de l'Amitié , pour avoir un
Morçeau de Métal jaune : Pauvre Homme, difois-
je , vous donnez trop pour votre Sifflet. -- Quand
j'ai rencontré un Homme de Plaifir , facrifiant tout
louable Perfectionnement de fon Ame , & toute
Amélioration de fon Etat aux Voluptés du Sens
purement corporel , & détruifant fa Santé dans
leur Pourfuite , Homme trompé , ai-je dit , vous
vous procurez des Peines au lieu des Plaifirs ; vous
payez trop pour votre Sifflet. -- Si j'en ai vu un
autre , entêté de beaux Habillemens , belles Maifons , beaux Meubles , beaux Equipages , tout
au-deffus de fa Fortune , qu'il ne fe procuroit qu'en
faifant des Dettes , & en allant finir fa Carriere
dans une Prifon ; Hélas ! ai-je dit , il a payé trop
pour fon Sifflet. -- Quand j'ai vu une très-belle
Fille , d'un Naturel bon & doux , mariée à un
Homme féroce & brutal , qui la maltraite conti-
nuellement ; C'eft grande Pitié , ai-je dit , qu'elle
ait tant payé pour un Sifflet ! -- Enfin j'ai conçu
que la plus grande Partie des Malheurs de l'Efpece
humaine viennent des Eftimations fauffes qu'on
fait de la Valeur des Chofes , & de ce qu'on donne
trop pour les Sifflets.

Néanmoins je fens que je dois avoir de la Charité pour ces Gens malheureux , quand je confidere
qu'avec toute la Sageffe dont je me vante , il y a cer-
taines Chofes dans ce bas Monde fi tentantes ; par
Exemple , les Pommes du Roi Jean , lefquelles
heureufement ne font pas à acheter ; car fi elles
étoient mifes à l'Enchere , je pourrois être très-

for your self instead of Pleasure, you pay too much for your Whistle. --If I see one fond of Appearance, of fine Cloaths, fine Houses, fine Furniture, fine Equipages, all above his Fortune, for which he contracts Debts, and ends his Career in a Prison ; *Alas,* says I, *he has paid too much for his Whistle.* --When I saw a beautiful sweet-temper'd Girl, marry'd to an ill-natured Brute of a Husband ; *What a Pity,* says I, *that she should pay so much for a Whistle !* --In short, I conceiv'd that great Part of the Miseries of Mankind, were brought upon them by the false Estimates they had made of the Value of Things, and by their *giving too much for the Whistle.*

Yet I ought to have Charity for these unhappy People, when I consider that with all this Wisdom of which I am boasting, there are certain things in the World so tempting ; for Example the Apples of King John, which happily are not to be bought, for if they were put to sale by Auction, I might very easily be led to ruin my self in the Purchase, and find that I had once more *given too much for the Whistle.*

Adieu, my dearest Friend, and believe me ever yours very sincerely and with unalterable Affection.

facilement porté à me ruiner par leur *Achat*, &
trouver que j'aurois encore une fois donné trop
pour le Sifflet.

Adieu, ma très-chere *Amie*, croyez-moi toujours le vôtre, bien *sincerement*, & avec une *Affection inaltérable.*

INFORMATION

TO THOSE

WHO WOULD REMOVE

TO AMERICA.

MANY Perfons in Europe having directly or by Letters, exprefs'd to the Writer of this, who is well acquainted with North-America, their Defire of tranfporting and eftablishing themfelves in that Country; but who appear to him to have formed thro' Ignorance, miftaken Ideas & Expectations of what is to be obtained there; he thinks it may be ufeful, and prevent inconvenient, expenfive & fruitlefs Removals and Voyages of improper Perfons, if he gives fome clearer & truer Notions of that Part of the World than appear to have hitherto prevailed.

He finds it is imagined by Numbers that the Inhabitants of North-America are rich, capable of rewarding, and difpos'd to reward all forts of Ingenuity; that they are at the fame time ignorant of all the Sciences; & confequently that ftrangers poffeffing Talents in the Belles-Letters, fine Arts, &c. muft be highly efteemed, and fo well paid as to become eafily rich themfelves; that there are alfo abundance of profitable Offices to be difpofed of,

A

which the Natives are not qualified to fill ; and that having few Persons of Family among them, Strangers of Birth must be greatly respected, and of course easily obtain the best of those Offices, which will make all their Fortunes : that the Goverments too, to encourage Emigrations from Europe, not only pay the expence of personal Transportation , but give Lands gratis to Strangers , with Negroes to work for them, Utensils of Husbandry, & Stocks of Cattle. These are all wild Imaginations ; and those who go to America with Expectations founded upon them, will surely find themselves disappointed.

The Truth is, that tho' there are in that Country few People so miserable as the Poor of Europe, there are also very few that in Europe would be called rich : it is rather a general happy Mediocrity that prevails. There are few great Proprietors of the Soil, and few Tenants ; most. People cultivate their own Lands, or follow some Handicraft or Merchandise ; very few rich enough to live idly upon their Rents or Incomes ; or to pay the high Prices given in Europe, for Paintings, Statues, Architecture and the other Works of Art that are more curious than useful. Hence the natural Geniuses that have arisen in America, with such Talents, have uniformly quitted that Country for Europe, where they can be more suitably rewarded. It is true that Letters and mathematical Knowledge are in Esteem there, but they are at the same time more common than is apprehended ; there being already existing nine Colleges or Universities, viz. four in New-England, and one in each of the Provinces of New-York, New-Jersey, Pensilvania, Maryland and Virginia, all furnish'd with learned Professors ; besides a number of smaller Academies : These educate many of their Youth

in the Languages and thofe Sciences that qualify
Men for the Profeffions of Divinity, Law or Phyfick.
Strangers indeed are by no means excluded from
exercifing thofe Profeffions, and the quick Increafe
of Inhabitants every where gives them a Chance of
Employ, which they have in common with the
Natives.   Of civil Offices or Employments there
are few ; no fuperfluous Ones as in Europe; and it
is a Rule eftablifh'd in fome of the States, that no
Office fhould be fo profitable as to make it defira-
ble.   The 36 Article of the Conftitution of Penfilvania , runs exprefly in thefe Words : *As every
Freeman, to preferve his Independance, (if he
has not a fufficient Eftate) ought to have fome
Profeffion, Calling , Trade or Farm, whereby he
may honeftly fubfift, there can be no Neceffity for,
nor Ufe in , eftablifhing Offices of Profit ; the
ufual Effects of which are Dependance and Servi-
lity, unbecoming Freemen, in the Poffeffors and
Expectants ; Faction , Contention , Corruption,
and Diforder among the People. Wherefore when-
ever an Office, thro' Increafe of Fees or otherwife,
becomes fo profitable as to occafion many to apply
for it, the Profits ought to be leffened by the Legif-
lature.*

Thefe Ideas prevailing more or lefs in all the
United States, it cannot be worth any Man's
while, who has a means of Living at home, to
expatriate himfelf in hopes of obtaining a profitable civil Office in America ; and as to military
Offices, they are at an End with the War ; the
Armies being disbanded. Much lefs is it advifea-
ble for a Perfon to go thither who has no other
Quality to recommend him but his Birth. In Europe it has indeed its Value, but it is a Commodity
that cannot be carried to a worfe Market than to
that of America, where People do not enquire

A 2

concerning a Stranger, *What is he?* but *What can he do?* If he has any useful Art, he is welcome ; and if he exercises it and behaves well, he will be respected by all that know him ; but a mere Man of Quality, who on that Account wants to live upon the Public, by some Office or Salary, will be despis'd and disregarded. The Husbandman is in honor there, & even the Mechanic, because their Employments are useful. The People have a Saying, that God Almighty is himself a Mechanic, the greatest in the Universe ; and he is respected and admired more for the Variety, Ingenuity and Utility of his Handiworks, than for the Antiquity of his Family. They are pleas'd with the Observation of a Negro, and frequently mention it, that *Boccarorra* (meaning the Whiteman) make de Blackman workee, make de Horse workee, make de Ox workee, make ebery ting workee ; only de Hog. He de Hog, no workee ; he eat, he drink, he walk about, he go to sleep when he pleafe, *he libb like a Gentleman.* According to these Opinions of the Americans, one of them would think himself more oblig'd to a Genealogist, who could prove for him that his Ancestors & Relations for ten Generations had been Ploughmen, Smiths, Carpenters, Turners, Weavers, Tanners, or even Shoemakers, & consequently that they were useful Members of Society ; than if he could only prove that they were Gentlemen, doing nothing of Value, but living idly on the Labour of others, mere *fruges consumere nati* *, and otherwise *good for nothing*, till by their Death, their Estates like the Carcase of the Negro's Gentleman-Hog, come to be *cut up.*

---

* *There are a Number of us born Merely to eat up the Corn.* WATTS.

With Regard to Encouragements for Strangers
from Government, they are really only what are
derived from good Laws & Liberty. Strangers are
welcome becaufe there is room enough for them all,
and therefore the old Inhabitants are not jealous of
them ; the Laws protect them fufficiently, fo that
they have no need of the Patronage of great Men ;
and every one will enjoy fecurely the Profits of his
Induftry. But if he does not bring a Fortune with
him, he muft work and be induftrious to live. One
or two Years Refidence give him all the Rights of a
Citizen ; but the Government does not at prefent,
whatever it may have done in former times, hire
People to become Settlers, by Paying their Paffages,
giving Land, Negroes, Utenfils, Stock, or any
other kind of Emolument whatfoever. In short
America is the Land of Labour, and by no means
what the English call *Lubberland,* and the French
Pays de Cocagne, where the Streets are faid to be
pav'd with half-peck Loaves, the Houfes til'd with
Pancakes, and where the Fowls fly about ready
roafted, crying, *Come eat me !*

Who then are the kind of Perfons to whom an
Emigration to America may be advantageous ? and
what are the Advantages they may reafonably
expect ?

Land being cheap in that Country, from the
vaft Forefts ftill void of Inhabitants, and not likely
to be occupied in an Age to come, infomuch that
the Propriety of an hundred Acres of fertile Soil
full of Wood may be obtained near the Frontiers
in many Places for eight or ten Guineas, hearty
young Labouring Men, who underftand the Huf-
bandry of Corn and Cattle, which is nearly the
fame in that Country as in Europe, may eafily eftablish themfelves there. A little Money fav'd of
the good Wages they receive there while they work

A 3

for others, enables them to buy the Land and begin their Plantation, in which they are assisted by the Good Will of their Neighbours and some Credit. Multitudes of poor People from England, Ireland, Scotland and Germany, have by this means in a few Years become wealthy Farmers, who in their own Countries, where all the Lands are fully occupied, and the Wages of Labour low, could never have emerged from the mean Condition whereinthey were born.

From the Salubrity of the Air, the Healthiness of the Climate, the Plenty of good Provisions, and the Encouragement to early Marriages, by the certainty of Subsistance in cultivating the Earth, the Increase of Inhabitants by natural Generation is very rapid in America, and becomes still more so by the Accession of Strangers; hence there is a continual Demand for more Artisans of all the necessary and useful kinds, to supply those Cultivators of the Earth with Houses, and with Furniture & Utensils of the grosser Sorts which cannot so well be brought from Europe. Tolerably good Workmen in any of those mechanic Arts, are sure to find Employ, and to be well paid for their Work, there being no Restraints preventing Strangers from exercising any Art they understand, nor any Permission necessary. If they are poor, they begin first as Servants or Journeymen; and if they are sober, industrious & frugal, they soon become Masters, establish themselves in Business, marry, raise Families, and become respectable Citizens.

Also, Persons of moderate Fortunes and Capitals, who having a Number of Children to provide for, are desirous of bringing them up to Industry, and to secure Estates for their Posterity, have Opportunities of doing it in America, which Europe does not afford. There they may be taught & prac-

tice profitable mechanic Arts, without incurring
Difgrace on that Account; but on the contrary
acquiring Refpect by fuch Abilities. There fmall
Capitals laid out in Lands, which daily become
more valuable by the Increafe of People, afford a
folid Profpect of ample Fortunes thereafter for
thofe Children. The Writer of this has known
feveral Inftances of large Tracts of Land, bought
on what was then the Frontier of Penfilvania, for
ten Pounds per hundred Acres, which, after twenty
Years, when the Settlements had been extended far
beyond them, fold readily, without any Improvement made upon them, for three Pounds per Acre.
The Acre in America is the fame with the English
Acre or the Acre of Normandy.

Thofe who defire to underftand the State of
Government in America, would do well to read
the Conftitutions of the feveral States, and the
Articles of Confederation that bind the whole together for general Purpofes under the Direction of
one Affembly called the Congrefs. Thefe Conftitutions have been printed by Order of Congrefs in
America; two Editions of them have alfo been
printed in London, and a good Tranflation of them
into French has lately been published at Paris.

Several of the Princes of Europe having of late
Years, from an Opinion of Advantage to arife by
producing all Commodities & Manufactures within
their own Dominions, fo as to diminish or render
ufelefs their Importations, have endeavoured to
entice Workmen from other Countries, by high
Salaries, Privileges, &c. Many Perfons preten-
ding to be skilled in various great Manufactures,
imagining that America muft be in Want of them,
and that the Congrefs would probably be difpos'd
to imitate the Princes above mentioned, have propofed to go over, on Condition of having their Paf-

A 4

fages paid, Lands given, Salaries appointed, ex-
clufive Privileges for Terms of Years, &c. Such
Perfons on reading the Articles of Confederation
will find that the Congrefs have no Power committed to them, or Money put into their Hands, for
fuch purpofes; and that if any fuch Encouragement is given, it muft be by the Government of fome
feparate State. This however has rarely been done
in America; and when it has been done it has rarely
fucceeded, fo as to eftablish a Manufacture which
the Country was not yet fo ripe for as to encourage
private Perfons to fet it up ; Labour being generally too dear there, & Hands difficult to be kept
together, every one defiring to be a Mafter, and the
Cheapnefs of Land enclining many to leave Trades
for Agriculture. Some indeed have met with Suc-
cefs, and are carried on to Advantage ; but they
are generally fuch as require only a few Hands, or
wherein great Part of the Work is perform'd by Machines. Goods that are bulky, & of fo fmall Value
as not well to bear the Expence of Freight, may
often be made cheaper in the Country than they
can be imported ; and the Manufacture of fuch
Goods will be profitable wherever there is a fufficient Demand. The Farmers in America produce
indeed a good deal of Wool & Flax ; and none is
exported, it is all work'd up ; but it is in the Way
of Domeftic Manufacture for the Ufe of the Family. The buying up Quantities of Wool & Flax
with the Defign to employ Spinners, Weavers, &c.
and form great Eftablishements, producing Quantities of Linen and Woollen Goods for Sale, has
been feveral times attempted in different Provinces ;
but thofe Projects have generally failed, Goods of
equal Value being imported cheaper. And when
the Governments have being folicited to fupport
fuch Schemes oy Encouragements, in Money, or

by impofing Duties an Importation of fuch Goods,
it has been generally refufed, on this Principle,
that if the Country is ripe for the Manufacture,
it may be carried on by private Perfons to Advantage; and if not, it is a Folly to think of forceing
Nature. Great Eftablishments of Manufacture, require great Numbers of Poor to do the Work for
fmall Wages; thefe Poor are to be found in Europe,
but will not be found in America, till the Lands
are all taken up and cultivated, and the excefs of
People who cannot get Land, want Employment.
The Manufacture of Silk, they fey, is natural in
France, as that of Cloth in England, becaufe each
Country produces in Plenty the firft Material : But
if England wil have a Manufacture of Silk as well
as that of Cloth, and France one of Cloth as well
as that of Silk, thefe unnatural Operations muft be
fupported by mutual Prohibitions or high Duties
on the Importation of each others Goods, by which
means the Workmen are enabled to tax the home-
Confumer by greater Prices, while the higher
Wages they receive makes them neither happier
nor richer, fince they only drink more and work
lefs. Therefore the Governments in America do
nothing to encourage fuch Projects. The People by
this Means are not impos'd on, either by the Merchant or Mechanic ; if the Merchant demands too
much Profit on imported Shoes, they buy of the
Shoemaker : and if he asks to high a Price, they
take them of the Merchant : thus the two Profeffions are Checks on each other. The Shoemaker
however has on the whole a confiderable Profit
upon his Labour in America, beyond what he had
in Europe, as he can add to his Price a Sum nearly
equal to all the Expences of Freight & Commiffion,
Rifque or Infurance, &c. neceffarily charged by
the Merchant, And the Cafe is the fame with the

Workmen in every other Mechanic Art. Hence it
is that Artisans generally live better and more easily
in America than in Europe, and such as are good
Œconomists make a comfortable Provision for Age,
& for their Children. Such may therefore remove
with Advantage to America.

In the old longsettled Countries of Europe, all
Arts, Trades, Professions, Farms, &c. are so full
that it is difficult for a poor Man who has Children, to place them where they may gain, or learn
to gain a decent Livelihood. The Artisans, who
fear creating future Rivals in Business, refuse to
take Apprentices, but upon Conditions of Money,
Maintenance or the like, which the Parents are
unable to comply with. Hence the Youth are
dragg'd up in Ignorance of every gainful Art, and
oblig'd to become Soldiers or Servants or Thieves,
for a Subsistance. In America the rapid Increase
of Inhabitants takes away that Fear of Rivalship,
& Artisans willingly receive Apprentices from the
hope of Profit by their Labour during the Remainder of the Time stipulated after they shall be instructed. Hence it is easy for poor Families to get
their Children instructed; for the Artisans are so
desirous of Apprentices, that many of them will
even give Money to the Parents to have Boys from
ten to fifteen Years of Age bound Apprentices to
them till the Age of twenty one; and many poor
Parents have by that means, on their Arrival in
the Country, raised Money enough to buy Land
sufficient to establish themselves, and to subsist the
rest of their Family by Agriculture. These Contracts for Apprentices are made before a Magistrate,
who regulates the Agreement according to Reason
and Justice; and having in view the Formation of
a future useful Citizen, obliges the Master to engage
by a written Indenture, not only that during the

time of Service ftipulated, the Apprentice shall be
duly provided with Meat, Drink, Apparel, wash-
ing & Lodging, and at its Expiration with a
compleat new fuit of Clothes, but alfo that he shall
be taught to read, write & caft Accompts, & that
he shall be well inftructed in the Art or Profeffion
of his Mafter, or fome other, by which he may
afterwards gain a Livelihood, and be able in his
turn to raife a Family. A Copy of this Indenture
is given to the Apprentice or his Friends, & the
Magiftrate keeps a Record of it, to which Recourfe
may be had, in cafe of Failure by the Mafter in
any Point of Performance. This Defire among the
Mafters to have more Hands employ'd in working
for them, induces them to pay the Paffages of
young Perfons, of both Sexes, who on their Arrival
agree to ferve them one, two, three or four Years ;
thofe who have already learnt a Trade agreeing for
a shorter Term in Proportion to their Skill and the
confequent immediate Value of their Service; and
thofe who have none, agreeing for a longer Term,
in Confideration of being taught an Art their Po-
verty would not permit them to acquire in their
own Country.

The almoft general Mediocrity of Fortune that
prevails in America, obliging its People to follow
fome Bufinefs for Subfiftance, thofe Vices that arife
ufually from Idlenefs are in a great Meafure preven-
ted. Induftry and conftant Employment are great
Prefervatives of the Morals and Virtue of a Nation.
Hence bad Examples to Youth are more rare in
America, which muft be a comfortable Confideration to Parents. To this may be truly added,
that ferious Religion under its various Denomina-
tions, is not only tolerated but refpected and practifed. Atheifm is unknown there, Infidelity rare
& fecret, fo that Perfons may live to a great Age

in that Country without having their Piety shock'd by meeting with either an Atheist or an Infidel. And the Divine Being seems to have manifested his Approbation of the mutual Forbearance and Kindness with which the different Sects treat each other, by the remarkable Prosperity with which he has been pleased to favour the whole Country.

AVERTISSEMENT
DU TRADUCTEUR.

*M*ADAME B.. *est une Dame fort aimable, & qui possede un talent distingué pour la Musique ; elle demeure à Passy où elle est en société avec M. Franklin. Ils avoient dans l'été de 1778 été passés ensemble une journée au* Moulin-Joly *où ce même jour volti-geoit sur la riviere un essaim de ces petites mouches que l'on nomme* Ephemeres, *& que le peuple appelle de la Manne. M. Franklin les examina avec attention, & envoya le lendemain à Madame B.. la lettre dont voici la traduction :*

*V*OUS pouvez, ma chere Amie, vous rappeller que, lorsque nous passâmes dernierement cette heureuse journée dans les jardins délicieux & la douce société du Moulin-Joly, je m'arrêtai dans une des promenades que nous fimes, & que je laissai la compagnie la continuer quelque temps sans moi.

On nous avoit montré un nombre infini de cadavres d'une petite espece de mouche que l'on nomme Ephemere, dont on nous dit que toutes les générations successives étoient nées & mortes dans le même jour. Il m'arriva d'en remarquer sur une feuille une compagnie vivante qui faisoit la conversation.

Vous savez que j'entends tous les langages

*

des efpeces inférieures à la notre: Ma trop
grande application à leur étude eft la meilleure
excufe que je puiffe donner du peu de progrès que j'ai fait dans votre langue charmante.
La curiofité me fit écouter les propos de ces
petites créatures ; mais la vivacité propre à
leur nation les faifant parler trois ou quatre à
la fois , je ne pus tirer prefque rien de leurs
difcours. Je compris cependant par quelques
expreffions interrompues que je faififfois de
temps en temps, qu'ils difputoient avec chaleur fur le mérite de deux Muficiens étrangers,
l'un un Coufin & l'autre un Bourdon. Ils paf-
foient leur temps dans ces débats , avec l'air
de fonger auffi peu à la briéveté de la vie que
s'ils en avoient été affurés pour un mois. Heureux peuple, me dis-je, vous vivez certainement fous un gouvernement fage , équitable
& modéré , puifqu'aucun grief public n'excite
vos plaintes , & que vous n'avez de fujet de
conteftation que la perfection ou l'imperfection d'une mufique étrangere.

Je les quittai pour me tourner vers un vieil-
lard à cheveux blancs , qui feul fur une autre
feuille fe parloit à lui-même. Son foliloque
m'amufa ; je l'ai écrit dans l'efperance qu'il
amufera de même celle à qui je dois le plus
fenfible des plaifirs, celui des charmes de fa
fociété & de l'harmonie célefte des fons qui
naiffent fous fa main.

« C'étoit , difoit-il, l'opinion des favans

» Philofophes de notre race qui ont vécu &
» fleuri long-temps avant le préfent âge,
» que ce vafte monde (1) ne pourroit pas
» lui-même fubfifter plus de dix-huit heu-
» res ; & je penfe que cette opinion n'étoit
» pas fans fondement, puifque par le mou-
» vement apparent du grand Luminaire qui
» donne la vie à toute la nature, & qui de
» mon temps a d'une maniere fenfible confi-
» dérablement décliné vers l'océan (2) qui
» borne cette terre, il faut qu'il termine fon
» cours à cette époque, s'éteigne dans les
» eaux qui nous environnent, & livre le
» monde à des glaces & des ténebres qui ame-
» neront néceffairement une mort & une def-
» truction univerfelle. J'ai vécu fept heures
» dans ces dix-huit ; c'eft un grand âge ; ce
» n'eft pas moins de quatre cents vingt minu-
» tes ; combien peu entre nous parviennent
» auffi loin ? J'ai vu des générations naître,
» fleurir & difparoître. Mes amis préfens font
» les enfans & les petits-enfans des amis de ma
» jeuneffe, qui hélas ! ne font plus, & je dois
» bientôt les fuivre; car par le cours ordinaire
» de la nature je ne puis m'attendre, quoi-
» qu'en bonne fanté, à vivre encore plus de
» fept à huit minutes : que me fervent à pré-
» fent tous mes travaux, toutes mes fatigues
» pour faire fur cette feuille une provifion de
» miellée, que je ne puis vivre affez pour con-

---

(1) Le Moulin-Joly. (2) La riviere de Seine.

» sommer ? Que me servent les débats poli-
» tiques dans lesquels je me suis engagé pour
» l'avantage de mes compatriotes , habitans
» de ce buisson ; ou mes recherches philoso-
» phiques consacrées au bien de notre espece
» en général ? En Politique que peuvent les
» loix sans les mœurs (1) ? Le cours des minu-
» tes rendra la génération présente des Ephe-
» meres aussi corrompue que celle des autres
» buissons plus anciens , & par conséquent
» aussi malheureux ; & en Philosophie que
» nos progrès sont lents ? Helas ! l'art est long
» & la vie est courte (2). Mes amis vou-
» droient me consoler par l'idée d'un nom
» qu'ils disent que je laisserai après moi. Ils
» disent que j'ai assez vécu pour ma gloire &
» pour la nature ; mais que sert la renommée
» pour un Ephemere qui n'existe plus ? Et
» l'histoire que deviendra-t-elle , lorsqu'à la
» dix-huitieme heure le monde lui-même , le
» Moulin-Joly tout entier , sera arrivé à sa
» fin pour n'être plus qu'un amas de ruines.

» Pour moi , après tant de recherches acti-
» ves , il ne reste de bien réel que la satisfac-
» tion d'avoir passé ma vie dans l'intention
» d'être utile , la conversation aimable d'un
» petit nombre de bonnes Dames Ephemeres,
» & de temps en temps le doux sourire &
» quelques accords de la toujours aimable
» *Brillante* ».

---

(1) Quid leges sine moribus? Hor. (2) Hipocrate.

M. F--n a Madame H--s.

CHAGRIN de votre barbare Refolution, prononcée fi pofitivement hier au Soir, de refter feule
toute votre Vie en l'Honneur de votre cher Mari,
je me retirai chez moi, je me jettai fur mon Lit, me
croyant mort, & je me trouvai dans les Champs
Elifées.

On me demanda fi j'avois envie de voir quelques
Perfonnages particuliers. Menez-moi chez les Thi-
lofophes. --Il y en a deux qui demeurent ici-près
dans ce Jardin : ils font de très-bons Voifins, &
très Amis l'un de l'autre. --Qui font-ils? --Socrate
& H****. --Je les eftime prodigieufement tous
les deux ; mais faites-moi voir premierement H****,
parce que j'entends un peu de François & pas un
mot de Grec. Il me reçut avec beaucoup de Courtoifie, m'ayant connu, difoit-il, de Réputation il
y avoit quelque Temps. Il me demanda mille Chofes fur la Guerre, & fur l'Etat préfent de la Religion, de la Liberté, & du Gouvernement en France.
--Vous ne vous informez donc pas de votre chere
Amie Madame H****; cependant elle vous aime
encore exceffivement, & il n'y a qu'une Heure que
j'étois chez elle. Ah! dit-il, vous me faites reffouvenir de mon ancienne Félicité. --Mais il faut
l'oublier pour être heureux ici. Pendant plufieurs
des premieres Années, je n ai penfé qu'à elle. Enfin
je fuis confolé. J'ai pris une autre Femme. --La
plus femblable à elle que je pouvois trouver. Elle
n'eft pas, il eft vrai, tout-à-fait fi belle, mais elle
a autant de bon Sens, un peu plus d'Efprit, & elle
m'aime infiniment. Son Etude continuelle eft de me
plaire ; & elle eft allée actuellement chercher le
meilleur Nectar & la meilleure Ambrofie pour me
regaler ce Soir ; reftez avec moi & vous la verrez.

J'apperçois, dis-je, que votre ancienne Amie est
plus fidelle que vous : car on lui a offert plusieurs
bons Partis qu'elle a refusés tous.   Je vous confesse
que je l'ai aimée, moi, à la Folie ; mais elle étoit
dure à mon Egard, & elle m'a rejetté absolument
pour l'Amour de vous.   Je vous plains, dit-il, de
votre Malheur ; car vraiment c'est une bonne &
belle Femme & bien aimable.   Mais l'Abbé de la
R****, & l'Abbé M****, ne font-ils pas encore
quelquefois chez elle ? Oui assurement ; car elle
n'a pas perdu un seul de vos Amis.   -- Si vous
aviez engagé l'Abbé M * * * * (en lui donnant du
Caffé à la Crême) à parler pour vous, peut-être
vous auriez réussi ; car il est Raisonneur subtil comme Duns Scotus ou St. Thomas ; il met ses Argu-
mens en si bon Ordre qu'ils deviennent presque irré-
sistibles ; ou bien en faisant présent à l'Abbé de la
R * * * * de quelque belle Edition d'un vieux Auteur
Classique, vous auriez obtenu qu'il parlât contre
vous ; & cela auroit encore mieux réussi : car j'ai
toujours observé, que, quand il conseille quelque
Chose, elle a un Penchant très-fort à faire le contraire.   -- A ces Mots entra la nouvelle Madame
H * * * * avec le Nectar : à l'Instant je reconnus en
elle Madame F * * * *, mon ancienne Amie Améri-
caine.   Je la réclamai.   Mais elle me dit froidement, j'ai été votre bonne Femme quarante-neuf
Années & quatre Mois, presqu'un demi Siécle ;
soyez content de cela.   J'ai formé ici une nouvelle
Chaîne, qui durera l'Eternité.

Fâché de ce Refus de mon Euridice, je pris tout
de suite la Resolution de quitter ces Ombres ingra-
tes, de revenir en ce bon Monde, revoir le Soleil &
vous. Me voici ! Vengeons-nous.

PARABOLE

CONTRE LA PERSECUTION,

A L'IMITATION DU LANGAGE
DE L'ECRITURE.

1. Et ensuite il arriva qu'Abraham étoit assis à la porte de sa tente vers le coucher du soleil.

2. Et il apperçut un homme courbé sous le poids des années, venant du désert appuyé sur un bâton.

3. Et Abraham se leva & alla au-devant de cet homme, & lui dit, viens dans ma tente, je t'en prie, & lave tes pieds, & demeure y toute la nuit, & tu te leveras demain du grand matin, & tu continueras ta route.

4. Et l'homme dit, non; car je resterai sous cet arbre.

5. Mais Abraham le pressa tant, qu'il se détourna; & ils arriverent à la tente : Et Abraham fit cuire un pain sans levain, & ils mangerent.

6. Et quand Abraham vit que cet homme ne bénissoit point Dieu, il lui dit; pourquoi n'adores-tu pas le Dieu très-haut créateur du ciel & de la terre ?

7. Et l'homme répondit, je n'adore point ton Dieu, & je n'invoque point son nom; parce que je me suis fait un Dieu, qui habite toujours dans ma maison & pourvoit à tous mes besoins.

*

8. Et le zele d'Abraham s'alluma contre cet homme, & il ſe leva & ſe jetta ſur lui & le conduiſit ainſi en le maltraitant juſqu'au déſert.

9. Et au milieu de la nuit Dieu appella A-braham, en diſant, Abraham, où eſt l'étranger?

10. Et Abraham répondit & dit, Seigneur, il ne vous adore point, & il n'invoque pas votre nom ; c'eſt pourquoi que je l'ai chaſſé de ma préſence juſque dans le déſert.

11. Et Dieu dit, ne l'ai-je pas ſouffert cent quatre-vingt-dix-huit ans, & ne l'ai-je pas nourri & habillé malgré ſa rebellion contre moi ; ne pouvois-tu pas, homme pécheur toi-même, le ſupporter une ſeule nuit ?

12. Et Abraham dit, que la colere de mon Seigneur ne s'allume pas contre ſon ſerviteur. Voilà que j'ai péché devant vous, pardonnez-moi, je vous prie.

13. Et Abraham ſe leva & courut au déſert, & chercha l'homme avec empreſſement, & le trouva ; & il retourna avec lui dans ſa tente ; & après l'avoir traité avec amitié, il le renvoya le lendemain avec des préſens.

14. Et Dieu parla une ſeconde fois à Abra-ham & lui dit, parce que tu as péché, j'affligerai ta poſtérité pendant quatre cents ans dans une terre étrangere :

51. Mais parce que tu t'es repenti, je la délivrerai, & je l'en ferai ſortir avec puiſſance & joie, & avec de grandes richeſſes.

LE SAGE ET LA GOUTTE.

Un fléau des plus redoutable,
La Goutte, ce mal incurable,
Chez un Sage alla se loger,
Et pensa le désespérer :
Il se plaignit. La sagesse a beau faire,
Alors qu'on souffre, on ne l'entend plus guère :
A la fin cependant, la raison l'emporta.
Contre le mal mon Sage disputa :
Chacun employa l'éloquence
Pour se prouver qu'il avoit tort.
La Goutte disoit ; la prudence,
Mon cher Docteur, n'est pas ton fort ;
Tu manges trop, tu convoites les femmes,
Tu ne promenes plus, & tu passes ton temps
Aux échecs, & par fois aux dames ;
Tu bois un peu. Dans ces doux passe-temps
L'humeur s'amasse, & c'est un grand service
De venir t'en débarrasser.
Tu devrois m'en remercier ;
Mais depuis un long tems je connois l'injustice.
Le Sage reprit à son tour
Et dit : Je l'avouerai, les attraits de l'amour

Le Sage & la Goutte.

De l'auftere raifon tolerant la rudeffe
Semblent prolonger la jeuneffe.
J'aime, j'aimai & j'aimerai toujours;
On m'aime auffi. Dois-je paffer mes jours
A me priver? Non, non, la vraie fageffe
Eft de jouir des biens que le ciel nous donna;
Un peu de punch; — une jolie Maîtreffe;
Deux quelquefois, — trois, — quatre, & ceter a:
De toutes celles à qui je pourrai plaire
Aucunes ne m'échappera:
Ma femme me le pardonna;
Et tu voudrois ici trancher de la févere.
Pour les échecs, fi j'y fuis le plus fort,
Je m'y complais; mais lorfque par caprice
Fortune fuit, ils m'ennuyent à la mort,
Et j'en ferois alors le facrifice —.
Par le fecours de la Philofophie,
Tout Sage ainfi fçait borner fes defirs,
Se confoler des peines de la vie.
Dupes & fots renoncent aux plaifirs.

M. F. a Madame la Fr—é.

Ma Foi, vous avez bien fait, Madame, de ne pas venir si loin, dans une Saison si rude, chercher un si triste Déjeuner. Mon Fils & moi nous n'avons pas été si sages. Je vais vous en donner l'Histoire.

Comme l'Invitation étoit pour onze Heures, & que vous étiez de la Partie, je m'imaginois trouver un Déjeuner dînatoire ; qu'il y auroit beaucoup de Monde ; que nous aurions non-seulement du Thé, mais du Caffé, du Chocolat, peut-être un Jambon, & plusieurs autres bonnes Choses. Je pris la Resolution d'y aller à Pied ; mes Souliers étoient un peu trop étroits ; j'arrivai presque estropié. En entrant dans la Cour, je fus un peu surpris de la trouver si vuide de Voitures, & de voir que nous étions les premiers venus. Nous montons l'Escalier. Point de Bruit. Nous entrons dans la Salle du Déjeuner. Personne que M. l'Abbé & M. C**** — Le Déjeuner fini, & mangé ! — Rien sur la Table que quelques Restes de Pain, & un peu de Beurre. On crie ; on court dire à Madame H***** que nous étions venus déjeuner. Elle quitte sa Toilette, elle vient demi-coeffée. On est surpris que je sois venu, quand vous m'avez écrit que vous ne

viendrez pas. Je nie le Fait. Pour le prouver, on me produit votre Lettre qu'ils ont
reçue & gardée.

Enfin un nouveau Déjeuner est ordonné.
L'un court pour de l'Eau fraîche, un autre
pour des Charbons. On souffle vigoureuse-
ment. J'avois grand Faim ; il étoit si tard ;
*une Marmite regardée est bien long-temps à
bouillir*, comme dit le bon Homme Richard.
Madame part pour Paris & nous quitte.
Nous commençons à manger. Le Beurre est
bientôt fini. M. l'Abbé demande si nous en
voulons encore ? Oui, assurement. Il sonne.
Personne ne vient. Nous causons ; il oublie
le Beurre. Je grattois l'Assiette ; alors il la
saisit, & court à la Cuisine en chercher.
Après quelque Temps il revient lentement,
disant tristement, il n'y en a plus dans la
Maison. Pour m'amuser, M. l'Abbé me propose une Promenade ; mes pieds s'y refusent.
En Conséquence nous laissons-là le Déjeuner;
& nous montons chez lui pour trouver de
quoi finir notre Repas avec ses bons Livres —.

Moi, tout désolé, ayant reçu seulement
au lieu d'une demi-Douzaine de vos doux
Baisers, affectionnés & substantiels, & fortement imprimés, que j'attendois de votre
Charité, l'Ombre d'un seul, donné par
Madame H*****, avec bonne grace, il est
vrai, mais le plus léger & superficiel qu'on
puisse imaginer.

M. F--n a Madame H--s.

CHAGRINÉ de votre Refolution barbare, prononcée fi pofitivement hier au foir, de refter feule pendant la vie en l'honneur de votre cher mari, je me retirois chez moi, tombois fur mon lit me croyant mort, & je me trouvois dans les Champs Elifées.

On m'a demandé fi j'avois l'envie de voir quelques Perfonages particuliers. Menez moi chez les Philofophes. — Il y en a deux qui demeurent ici près dans ce Jardin : Ils font de très-bons voifins, & très-Amis l'un de l'autre. --Qui font ils ? --Socrate & H****. --Je les eftime prodigieufement tous les deux; mais faitez moi voir premierement H****, parce que j'entends un peu de François & pas un mot de Grecque. --Il m'a reçu avec beaucoup de courtoifie, m'ayant connu, difoit-il, de reputation il y a quelque temps. Il m'a demandé mille chofes fur la Guerre, & fur l'état préfent de la Religion, de la Liberté, & du Gouvernement en France. --Vous ne demandez rien donc de votre chere Amie Madame H*****; & cependant elle vous aime encore exceffivement, & il n'y a qu'une heure que j'étois chez elle. Ah! dit il, vous me faites reffouvenir de mon ancienne Félicité. --Mais il faut l'oublier pour être heureux ici. Pendant plufieurs des premieres années, je n'ai penfé qu'à elle. Enfin je fuis confolé. J'ai pris une autre Femme. --La plus femblable à elle que je pouvois trouver. Elle n'eft pas, c'eft vrai, tout-a-fait fi belle, mais elle a autant de bon fens, un peu plus d'efprit, & elle m'aime infiniment. Son étude continuelle eft de me plaire ; & elle eft fortie actuellement chercher le meilleur Nectar & Ambrofie pour me regaler ce foir ; Reftez avec moi & vous la verrez. J'apperçois, difois-je, que votre ancienne Amie eft plus fidelle que vous : **Car**

plufieurs bons Partis lui ont été offerts qu'elle a refu-
fés tous. Je vous confeffe que je l'ai aimée, moi, à la
folie ; mais elle étoit dure à mon égard , & m'a re-
jeté abfolument pour l'amour de vous. Je vous
plains , dit-il , de votre malheur ; car vraiment c'eft
une bonne & belle femme & bien aimable. Mais
l'Abbé de la R****, & l'Abbé M****, ne font ils
pas encore quelquefois chez elle ? Oui affurement ;
car elle n'a pas perdu un feul de vos Amis. -- Si
vous aviez gagné l'Abbé M**** (avec le Caffé à la
Crème) de parler pour vous , peut-être vous auriez
reuffi ; car il eft Raifoneur fubtil comme Duns Scotus
ou St. Thomas ; il met fes Arguments en fi bon
Ordre qu'ils dèviennent prefque irréfiftibles. Auffi fi
l'Abbé de la R**** a été gagné (par quelque belle
Edition d'un vieux Claffique) à parler contre vous ,
cela auroit été mieux : car j'ai toujours obfervé , que
quand il confeille quelque chofe , elle a un penchant
très-fort à faire le revers. -- A ces mots entroit la
nouvelle Madame H **** avec le Neftar : A l'inf-
tant je l'ai reconue être Madame F****, mon ancienne Amie Americaine. Je l'ai reclamée. Mais
elle me difoit froidement, J'ai été votre bonne Femme quarante-neuf années & quatre Mois, prefqu'un
demi fiecle ; foyez content de cela. J'ai formé
ici une nouvelle Conneftion, qui durera à l'Eternité.

Déplu de ce Refus de mon Euridice, je prenois
tout de fuite la Refolution de quitter ces Ombres in-
grates, de revenir en ce bon Monde, revoir le Soleil
& vous. Me voici ! Vengeons nous..

REMARQUES

SUR LA POLITESSE

DES SAUVAGES

DE L'AMÉRIQUE SEPTENTRIONALE:

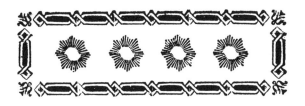

REMARQUES

ſUR LA POLIſTEſſE

DES SAUVAGES

DE L'AMÉRIQUE SEPTENTRIONALE.

Nous les appellons Sauvages parce que leurs Mœurs différent des nôtres, & que nous regardons nos Mœurs comme la Perfection de la Pòliteſſe ; ils ont préciſement la même Opinion des leurs.

Si nous examinions avec Impartialité les Mœurs des différentes Nations , peut - être trouverions-nous qu'il n'y a pas de Peuple ſi groſſier qu'il ſoit , qui n'ait quelques Regles de Politeſſe , ni de Peuple ſi poli qu'il ne conſerve quelques Reſtes de Groſſiéreté.

Les Indiens, lorſqu'ils ſont jeunes, ſont Chaſſeurs & Guerriers ; quand ils ſont vieux, ils deviennent Conſeillers ; car chez eux c'eſt

A

le Conseil ou l'Assemblée des Sages qui conſtitue le Gouvernement, & qui gouverne ſeulement par les Exhortations; il n'y a point de Force coactive, point de Priſon; il n'exiſte aucuns Officiers chargés de forcer à l'Obéiſſance ou d'infliger des Punitions. Cette Maniere de ſe gouverner les porte en général à étudier l'Art de la Parole, le meilleur Orateur ayant communément la plus grande influence.

Les Femmes Indiennes cultivent la Terre, apprêtent la Nourriture, nourriſſent & élevent les Enfans, & ce ſont elles encore qui conſervent & tranſmettent à la Poſtérité la Mémoire des Evénemens publics. Ils regardent ces Occupations des Hommes & des Femmes ainſi reparties comme naturelles & honorables. Ayant peu de Beſoins factices, ils ont beaucoup de Temps de reſte pour la Converſation, qui eſt pour eux le Moyen de cultiver & de perfectionner leur Eſprit. Notre Maniere de vivre laborieuſe & toujours occupée leur paroît baſſe & ſervile; & les Connoiſſances d'après leſquelles nous nous eſtimons nousmême ſont inutiles & frivoles à leurs Yeux.

Voici une Preuve de cette Opinion dans ce qui ſe paſſa lors du Traité conclu à Lancaſter en Penſylvanie dans l'Année 1744 entre le Gouvernement de Virginie & les Six-Nations. Après que les Affaires principales furent arrangées, les Commiſſaires Virginiens informerent les Indiens par un Difcours, qu'il y avoit dans le College de Williamsburg un Fond deftiné à l'Education des jeunes Indiens, & que, fi les Six-Nations vouloient envoyer à ce College une demi-Douzaine de jeunes Garçons, le Gouvernement prendroit Soin qu'ils fuffent pourvus de tout, & inftruits dans toutes les Connoiffances que l'on y donne aux jeunes Blancs. C'eft une des Regles de la Politeffe Indienne de ne pas répondre à une Propofition publique le Jour même qu'elle a été faite; ils penfent que ce feroit la traiter avec trop de Légéreté, & qu'ils témoignent beaucoup plus d'Egard en prenant du Temps pour l'examiner comme un Objet d'une grande Importance. Ils différent donc leur Réponfe jufques au Jour fuivant; alors leur Orateur commença par exprimer combien ils étoient pénétrés de l'Offre pleine de Bonté que le Gouvernement de Virginie faifoit à leurs Nations; car nous favons, dit-il, que vous faites le plus grand cas de l'Efpece de Connoiffance que l'on enfeigne dans ces Colleges, & que l'Entretien de nos jeunes Gens tant qu'ils feront chez vous fera très-difpendieux. Nous fommes donc convaincus qu'en nous faifant cette Offre, votre Intention eft de nous procurer un grand Bien, & nous vous en remercions de tout notre Cœur. Mais fages comme vous êtes, vous devez favoir que les différentes Nations ont des Idées différentes fur les mêmes Chofes, ainfi vous ne trouverez pas mauvais que les nôtres fur cette Efpece d'Education ne foient pas conformes à celles que vous en avez. Nous l'avons éprouvé plufieurs fois ; car plufieurs de nos jeunes Gens ont été ci-devant élevés dans les Colleges des Provinces Septentrionales ; ils ont été inftruits dans toutes vos Sciences ; mais lorfqu'ils font revenus chez nous, ils étoient mauvais Coureurs, ils ignoroient les Moyens de vivre dans les Bois, ils étoient incapables de fupporter le Froid & la Faim, ils ne favoient ni bâtir une Cabane, ni prendre un Daim, ni tuer un Ennemi ; ils parloient imparfaitement notre Langue : on ne pouvoit donc en faire ni de Chaffeurs, ni de Guerriers, ni de Confeillers ; ils n'étoient abfolument bons à rien. Mais quoique nous n'acceptent pas vos Offres, pleines de Bienveillance, nous ne vous en fommes pas moins obligés, & pour vous en temoigner notre Reconnoiffance, fi les principaux Habitans de Virginie veulent nous envoyer douze de leurs Enfans, nous prendrons grand Soin de leur Education ; nous les inftruirons dans toutes les Chofes que nous favons, & nous en ferons des *Hommes*.

Comme les Sauvages ont des Occafions fréquentes de tenir de Confeils, ils fe font accoutumés à maintenir dans ces Affemblées publiques beaucoup d'Ordre & une grande Décence; les Vieillards font affis au premier Rang,

les Guerriers au second, & les Femmes avec
les Enfans font au dernier. L'emploi & le
Devoir des Femmes font de remarquer avec
Attention & Exactitude tout ce qui s'y paffe,
afin de fe l'imprimer dans le Mémoire, car
l'Ecriture eft inconnue chez ces Peuples, &
de l'apprendre à leurs Enfans. Elles font, fi
l'on peut s'exprimer ainfi, les Régiftres du Con-
feil, & elles confervent par Tradition les Stipulations de Traités conclus cent ans auparavant, de Maniere que cette Tradition com-
parée avec nos Actes écrits s'y trouve toujours
exactement conforme. Celui qui veut parler
dans ces Confeils fe leve, les autres gardent
un profond Silence; quand il a fini & qu'il
s'affied, ils lui laiffent cinq ou fix Minutes
pour fe recueillir, afin que, s'il a oublié quelque Chofe, ou que, s'il a quelque Chofe à
ajouter, il puiffe fe lever de nouveau & ter-
miner à Loifir fon Difcours. C'eft chez eux
une très-grande Impoliteffe que d'interrom-
pre une Perfonne qui parle même dans la
Converfation ordinaire. Quelle Différence de
ces Confeils à la Chambre fi polie des Communes d'Angleterre, où à Peine il fe paffe
un Jour fans quelque Tumulte, au Milieu
duquel l'Orateur s'enroue à Force de crier à
l'Ordre ; & quelle Différence auffi de leurs
Converfations avec celles de beaucoup de So-
ciétés polies d'Europe, où le Bavardage impatient de ceux avec qui vous converfez, vous

coupe la Parole au Milieu de votre Phrafe, a moins que vous ne vous hâtiez de la débiter avec la plus grande Rapidité, & ne vous permet prefque jamais de la finir.

La Politeffe de ces Sauvages dans la Converfation eft effectivement portée à l'Excès, puifqu'elle leur fait une Regle de ne jamais nier ou contredire la Vérité de ce que l'on avance devant eux. Il eft vrai que par ce Moyen ils évitent les Difputes ; mais auffi il eft très-difficile de connoître leur Penfée & de découvrir l'Impreffion que l'on fait fur eux. Les Miffionnaires qui ont tenté de les convertir à la Religion Chrétienne fe plaignent tous de cette Habitude comme d'un des plus grands Obftacles au Succès de leur Miffion. Les Indiens écoutent avec Patience les Vérités de l'Evangile lorfqu'on les leur explique, & ils donnent leurs Témoignages ordinaires d'Affentiment & d'Approbation : vous les croyez convaincus ; mais point du tout, c'eft pure Politeffe.

Un Miniftre Suedois ayant affemblé les Chefs des Indiens de la Riviere Sufquehanah, leur fit un Sermon, dans lequel il leur développa les principaux Faits hiftoriques qui fervent de Bafe à notre Religion ; tels que la Chute de nos premiers Parens en mangeant la Pomme, la Venue du Chrift pour réparer le Mal qui en étoit réfulté, fes Miracles & fa Paffion, &c. Quand il eut fini, un des

Indiens ſe leva comme Orateur pour le remercier.

Tout ce que vous venez de nous dire eſt
très-bon , lui répondit-il ; il eſt effectivement
bien mal fait de manger des Pommes : ſans doute
il vaut beaucoup mieux les employer toutes
à faire du Cidre. Nous vous ſommes très-
obligés de la Bonté que vous avez eue de venir
d'auſſi loin pour nous conter ces Hiſtoires que
vous tenez de vos Meres : & je vais en Signe
de Reconnoiſſance vous raconter quelques-
unes de celles que les nôtres nous ont appriſes.
Au Commencement des Choſes, nos Peres n'a-
voient que la Chair des Animaux pour ſe
nourrir , & ſi leurs Chaſſes n'étoient pas heu-
reuſes, ils mouroient de Faim. Deux de nos
jeunes Chaſſeurs ayant tué un Daim, firent du
Feu dans les Bois pour en griller une Portion;
comme ils ſe diſpoſoient à ſatisfaire leur ap-
pétit , ils virent une belle & jeune Femme
deſcendre des Nuages , & s'aſſeoir ſur cette
Montagne que vous voyez de ce Côté au
Milieu des Montagnes bleues. C'eſt un Eſprit , ſe dirent-ils l'un à l'autre , qui peut-
être a ſenti griller notre Gibier , & qui
veut en manger , offrons lui en un Morçeau;
auſſi-tôt ils lui préſenterent la Langue. Le
Goût de ce Mets parut lui plaire , & elle leur
dit ; votre Honnêteté ſera récompenſée , re-
venez dans ce même Lieu après treize Lunes,
& vous y trouverez quelque Choſe qui vous
A 4

fera d'une grande Utilité pour vous nourrir, vous & vos Enfans jufques à la Poftérité la plus reculée.   Ils y revinrent , & à leur grand Etonnement, ils trouverent des Plantes qu'ils n'avoient jamais vues auparavant ; mais qui depuis ce Temps déja très-ancien , ont été toujours cultivées parmi nous avec beau-coup de Succès & d'Avantage.   Ils trouve-rent du *Mais* dans la Place où fa Main droite avoit touché la Terre ; des *Haricots* dans celle qui avoit été touchée de fa main gauche, & dans celle fur laquelle elle s'étoit affife ils trouverent du *Tabac*.   Le bon Miffionnaire, fort choqué de ce Conte ridicule, leur dit, les Chofes que je vous ai annoncées étoient des Vérités facrées ; mais toutes celles que vous me dites ne font que des Fables , de pu-res Fictions & des Fauffetés.   Mon Frere, répliqua l'Indien offenfé , il me femble que vos Parens ont été injuftes envers vous en ne vous donnant pas une bonne Education ; ils ne vous ont pas bien inftruit des Principes de la Civilité réciproque ; vous avez vu que nous qui entendons & pratiquons ces Regles, nous avons cru à toutes vos Hiftoires , pour-quoi refufez-vous de croire aux nôtres.

Lorfque quelques Sauvages Indiens vien-nent dans nos Villes, notre Peuple s'amaffe autour d'eux , les regarde avec Avidité , & les incommode par la Foule , tandis qu'ils fouhaiteroient être à leur aife entr'eux ou avec quelques Perſonnes en particulier : cet Effet de notre Curioſité leur paroît une Impoliteſſe , & ils l'attribuent au Défaut d'Inſtruction dans les premieres Regles de la Civilité & des bonnes Manieres. Nous ſommes , diſent-ils, tout auſſi curieux que vous , & lorſque vous venez dans nos Villages, nous avons tout autant d'envie de vous voir ; mais pour la ſatisfaire nous nous cachons derriere des Buiſſons auprès deſquels vous devez paſſer ; & nous ne nous précipitons jamais auprès ou au milieu de vous.

Leur Maniere d'entrer dans les Villages les uns des autres , a auſſi ſes Regles ; c'eſt un Manque de Politeſſe aux Etrangers qui voyagent d'entrer tout de ſuite dans un Village ſans donner Avis de leur Arrivée : Auſſi-tôt donc qu'ils en approchent à la Portée de la Voix , ils s'arrêtent , pouſſent un Cri , & reſtent juſques à ce qu'on les invite à y entrer. Communément deux Vieillards ſortent à leur Rencontre & les y introduiſent. Il y a dans chaque Village une Habitation toujours vacante que l'on appelle la Maiſon des Etrangers. On les y établit , tandis que les Vieillards s'en vont de Cabane en Cabane annoncer à tous les Habitans qu'il eſt arrivé des Etrangers , qu'ils ſont vraiſemblablement fatigués , & qu'ils ont Faim ; chacun auſſitôt leur envoie ce qu'il peut de Vivres , & de Peaux pour ſe coucher. Quand les Etrangers se sont rafraichis par le Repos & en prenant leurs Repas, on apporte des Pipes & du Tabac; & c'est alors, mais jamais auparavant, que s'établit la Conversation; elle commence par des Questions; qui êtes-vous, où allez-vous, quelles Nouvelles y a-t-il, etc. & communement elle finit par des Offres de Service. Si les Etrangers ont besoin des Guides, ou si leur faut quelque autre Chose pour continuer leur Voyage, on leur en fournit, et l'on ne leur demande rien pour toutes les Commodités qu'on leur a procurées.

Cette Hospitalité que l'on peut appeller publique, et qui est regardée chez eux comme une Vertu principale, est aussi pratiquée et avec autant de zele par les Particuliers; en voici un Exemple que je tiens de *Gonrad Weiser*, notre Interprete. Il avoit habité long-temps chez les Six-Nations, il y étoit pour ainsi dire naturalisé, et parloit fort bien la Langue Mohock; traversant un Jour le Pays des Indiens pour porter un Message de nos Gouverneurs au Conseil qui résidoit à *Onondaga*, il s'arrêta à l'Habitation de *Canassatego*, qui étoit une de ses anciennes Connoissances. Cet Indien l'embrassa, étendit des Fourrures pour l'y faire asseoir, lui présenta des Haricots bouillis et du Gibier, avec un Mêlange de Rum et d'Eau pour sa Boisson. Quand il se fut bien rafraîchi, et qu'il eut allumé sa Pipe, Canassatego commença la

Converſation, et lui demanda comment il s'é-
toit porté pendant le long-temps qu'ils avoient
paſſés ſans ſe voir , d'où il venoit à préſent,
quel étoit le Motif de ſon Voyage, etc. etc.
Conrad répondit à toutes ces Queſtions ; et
la Converſation commençant à tomber, l'Indien , pour la continuer , lui dit , Conrad,
vous avez vécu long-temps parmi les Blancs,
et vous connoiſſez un peu leurs Uſages et leurs
Mœurs ; j'ai été quelquefois à *Albany* , et
j'ai remarqué qu'un Jour ſur ſept ils ferment
leurs Boutiques et s'aſſemblent tous dans la
grande Maiſon ; pourquoi cela, dites-le moi,
et qu'eſt-ce qu'ils y font ? Ils s'y raſſemblent,
dit Conrad , pour écouter et apprendre de
bonnes choſes. Oh ! répliqua l'Indien , je
ne doute pas qu'ils ne vous l'aient dit ; ils
m'ont bien dit auſſi la même choſe ; mais je
révoque fort en Doute la Vérité de ce qu'ils
diſent , et je vais vous en expoſer mes Rai-
ſons.

J'allai dernierement à Albany pour vendre
mes Peaux , et pour acheter des Couvertures,
des Couteaux, de la Poudre , du Rum , etc.
vous ſavez que je faiſois ordinairement **Affaire**
avec *Hans Hanſon* ; mais j'eus quelque Envie cette fois d'eſſayer d'un autre Marchand :
cependant j'allai d'abord chercher Hans, et je
lui demandai ce qu'il me donneroit pour mes
Peaux de Caſtor. Il me répondit qu'il ne pourroit pas m'en donner plus de quatre Shellings la

Livre; mais, ajouta-t-il, je ne puis pas maintenant parler d'Affaire. Voici le Jour où nous nous rassemblons pour apprendre de bonnes Choses, et je vais à l'Assemblée. Hé bien, dis-je en moi-même, puisque nous ne pouvons pas faire Affaire aujourd'hui, je puis tout aussi-bien aller à l'Assemblée; et j'y allai avec lui. J'y vis un grand Homme habillé en noir, qui se tenoit debout, et qui parloit au Peuple avec l'Air fort en Colere; je n'entendois pas ce qu'il disoit; mais m'appercevant qu'il me regardoit beaucoup, et regardoit aussi Hanson, j'imaginai qu'il étoit en Colere de me voir là; je m'en allai donc, je m'assis auprès de la Maison, je battis mon Briquet et j'allumai ma Pipe en attendant que l'Assemblée finit. Je pensai aussi que l'Homme en noir avoit dit quelque chose des Castors, et je soupçonnai que ce Commerce pouvoit être le Sujet de leur Assemblée; aussi dès qu'ils sortirent, j'accostai mon Marchand; hé-bien Hans, lui dis-je, j'espere que vous êtes convenus de me payer plus de quatre Shellings la Livre. Non, répondit-il, je ne puis même plus en donner ce prix, je ne puis pas aller au-delà de trois Shellings et six Sols. Je m'adressai alors à plusieurs autres Marchands qui tous me chanterent la même Chanson. Trois Shellings et six Sols, trois Shellings et six Sols. Je vis alors bien clairement que mes Soupçons étoient fondés, que tout

ce qu'ils difoient des bonnes Chofes qu'ils
alloient apprendre dans leurs Affemblées, étoit
un vain Prétexte, et que leur véritable Objet
étoit d'avifer enfemble aux Moyens d'attraper
les Indiens fur le Prix des Caftors. Faites-y
un peu d'Attention, Conrad, et vous ferez
de mon Avis. Si c'étoit pour apprendre de
bonnes Chofes qu'ils s'affemblent auffi fouvent, ils devroient certainement en avoir appris un peu jufques à préfent : mais ils font
encore tout-à-fait Ignorans des bonnes Chofes.
Vous connoiffez nos Ufages. Si quelque
Blanc, voyageant dans notre Pays, entre dans
quelques-unes de nos Cabanes, nous le trai-
tons tous comme je vous traite, nous faifons
fecher fes Vêtemens s'ils font mouillés, nous
le faifons chauffer s'il a froid, nous lui donnons bien à boire et à manger pour qu'il
puiffe appaifer et fatisfaire fa Faim et fa Soif;
nous étendons de bonnes Fourrures pour qu'il
s'y couche et s'y repofe, et nous ne lui deman-
dons rien en Retour * ; mais moi, fi je vais

---

* C'eft une Chofe digne de Remarque, que dans
tous les Pays & dans tous les Siecles l'Hofpitalité
ait été reconnue pour la Vertu de ceux que les Nations civilifées ont jugé à propos d'appeller *Barbares.* Les Grecs ont célébré l'Hofpitalité des Scytes.
Les Sarrafins l'ont portée à un Degré éminent, &
cette Vertu regne encore aujourd'hui chez les Arabes
du Défert. Saint-Paul nous dit auffi dans la Relation de fon Voyage & de fon Naufrage dans l'Ifle

à Albany dans la Maiſon d'un Blanc, et ſi je demande à manger ou à boire, où eſt votre Argent, me diſent-ils; et ſi je n'en ai point, ils me diſent, allez-vous-en, Chien d'Indien. Vous voyez bien qu'ils n'ont pas encore appris ces premieres bonnes Choſes que nous ſavons tous ſans avoir beſoin d'Aſſemblées pour les apprendre, parce que nos Meres nous les ont enſeignées dès notre Enfance. Il eſt donc impoſſible ou que leurs Aſſemblées ſoient comme ils le prétendent pour cet Objet, où qu'elles aient un pareil Effet ; elles n'ont d'autre But que *d'inventer les Moyens d'at-traper les Indiens ſur le Prix des Caſtors.*

---

de Malte, *Les Barbares nous traiterent avec une Humanité peu commune ; car ils allumerent du Feu, & nous reçurent tous chez eux à cauſe de la Pluie qui tomboit, & à cauſe du Froid.*

REMARKS

CONCERNING THE SAVAGES

OF NORTH-AMERICA.

SAVAGES we call them, becaufe their manners differ from ours, which we think the Perfection of Civility ; they think the fame of theirs.

Perhaps if we could examine the manners of different Nations with Impartiality, we fhould find no People fo rude as to be without any Rules of Politenefs ; nor any fo polite as not to have fome remains of Rudenefs.

The Indian Men, when young, are Hunters and Warriors ; when old, Counfellors ; for all their Government is by the Counfel or Advice of the Sages ; there is no Force, there are no Prifons, no Officers to compel Obedience, or inflict Punifhment. Hence they generally ftudy Oratory ; the beft Speaker having the moft Influence. The Indian Women till the Ground, drefs the Food, nurfe and bring up the Children, and preferve and hand down to Pofterity the Memory of Public Tranfactions. Thefe Employments of Men and Women are accounted natural and honorable. Having few Artificial Wants, they have abundance of Leifure for Improvement by Converfation. Our laborious manner of Life compared with theirs, they efteem flavifh and bafe ; and the Learning on which we value ourfelves ; they regard as frivolous and ufelefs. An Inftance of this occurred at the Treaty of Lancafter in Pennfylvania, Anno 1744,

A

between the Government of Virginia & the Six Nations. After the principal Bufinefs was fettled,
the Commiffioners from Virginia acquainted the Indians by a Speech, that there was at Williamfburg
a College with a Fund for Educating Indian Youth,
and that if the Chiefs of the Six-Nations would fend
down half a dozen of their Sons to that College, the
Government would take Care that they fhould be
well provided for, and inftructed in all the Learning
of the white People. It is one of the Indian Rules
of Politenefs not to anfwer a public Propofition the
fame day that it is made; they think it would be
treating it as a light Matter; and that they fhow it
Refpect by taking time to confider it, as of a Matter
important. They therefore deferred their Anfwer
till the day following; when their Speaker began
by expreffing their deep Senfe of the Kindnefs of
the Virginia Government, in making them that
Offer; for we know, fays he, that you highly efteem the kind of Learning taught in thofe Colleges,
and that the Maintenance of our Young Men while
with you, would be very expenfive to you. We are
convinced therefore that you mean to do us good by
your Propofal, and we thank you heartily. But
you who are wife muft know, that different Nations have different Conceptions of things; and
you will therefore not take it amifs, if our Ideas
of this Kind of Education happen not to be the
fame with yours. We have had fome Experience
of it: Several of our Young People were formerly
brought up at the Colleges of the Northern Provinces; they were inftructed in all your Sciences; but
when they came back to us, they were bad Runners, ignorant of every means of living in the
Woods, unable to bear either Cold or Hunger,
knew neither how to build a Cabin, take a Deer,
or kill an Enemy, fpoke our Language imperfectly;
were therefore neither fit for Hunters, Warriors,

or Counfellors; they were totally good for nothing.
We are however not the lefs obliged by your kind
Offer, tho' we decline accepting it; and to show
our grateful Senfe of it, if the Gentlemen of Virginia will fend us a dozen of their Sons, we will
take great Care of their Education, inftruct them
in all we know, and make *Men* of them.

Having frequent Occafions to hold public Councils, they have acquired great Order and Decency
in conducting them. The old Men fit in the fore-
moft Ranks, the Warriors in the next, and the
Women and Children in the hindmoft. The Bufinefs
of the Women is to take exact notice of what paffes,
imprint it in their Memories, for they have no
Writing, and communicate it to their Children.
They are the Records of the Council, and they
preferve Tradition of the Stipulations in Treaties
a hundred Years back, which when we compare
with our Writings we always find exact. He that
would fpeak, rifes. The reft obferve a profound
Silence. When he has finifhed and fits down, they
leave him five or fix Minutes to recollect, that if he
has omitted any thing he intended to fay, or has
any thing to add, he may rife again and deliver it.
To interrupt another, even in common Converfation, is reckoned highly indecent. How different
this is from the Conduct of a polite British Houfe
of Commons, where fcarce a Day paffes without
fome Confufion that makes the Speaker hoarfe in
calling *to order;* and how different from the mode
of Converfation in many polite Companies of Europe, where if you do not deliver your Sentence
with great Rapidity, you are cut off in the middle
of it by the impatient Loquacity of thofe you converfe with, & never fuffer'd to finish it.

The Politenefs of thefe Savages in Converfation
is indeed carried to excefs, fince it does not permit
them to contradict, or deny the Truth of what is

A 2

aſſerted in their Preſence. By this means they indeed avoid Diſputes, but then it becomes difficult
to know their Minds, or what Impreſſion you
make upon them. The Miſſionaries who have attempted to convert them to Chriſtianity, all complain of this as one of the great Difficulties of their
Miſſion. The Indians hear with Patience the Truths
of the Goſpel explained to them, and give their
uſual Tokens of Aſſent and Approbation : you
would think they were convinced. No ſuch Matter.
It is mere Civility.

A Suediſh Miniſter having aſſembled the Chiefs
of the Saſquehanah Indians, made a Sermon to them,
acquainting them with the principal hiſtorical Facts
on which our Religion is founded, ſuch as the Fall
of our firſt Parents by Eating an Apple, the Coming
of Chriſt to repair the Miſchief, his Miracles and
Suffering, &c. When he had finiſhed, an Indian
Orator ſtood up to thank him. What you have told
us, ſays he, is all very good. It is indeed bad to
eat Apples. It is better to make them all into
Cyder. We are much obliged by your Kindneſs in
coming ſo far to tell us thoſe things which you
have heard from your Mothers. In Return I will
tell you ſome of thoſe we have heard from ours.

In the Beginning our Fathers had only the Fleſh
of Animals to ſubſiſt on, and if their Hunting was
unſucceſsful, they were ſtarving. Two of our
young Hunters having killed a Deer, made a Fire
in the Woods to broil ſome Parts of it. When they
were about to ſatisfy their Hunger, they beheld a
beautiful young Woman deſcend from the Clouds,
and ſeat herſelf on that Hill which you ſee yonder
among the blue Mountains. They ſaid to each
other, it is a Spirit that perhaps has ſmelt our broiling Veniſon, & wiſhes to eat of it : let us offer
ſome to her. They preſented her with the Tongue :
She was pleaſed with the Taſte of it, & ſaid, your

Kindnefs shall be rewarded. Come to this Place after thirteen Moons, and you shall find fomething that will be of great Benefit in nourishing you and your Children to the lateft Generations. They did fo, and to their Surprife found Plants they had never feen before, but which from that ancient time have been conftantly cultivated among us to our great Advantage. Where her right Hand had touch'd the Ground, they found Maize; where her left Hand had touch'd it, they found Kidney-beans; and where her Backfide had fat on it, they found Tobacco. The good Miffionary, difgufted with this idle Tale, faid, what I delivered to you were facred Truths; but what you tell me is mere Fable, Fiction & Falfehood. The Indian offended, reply'd, my Brother, it feems your Friends have not done you Juftice in your Education; they have not well inftructed you in the Rules of common Civility. You faw that we who underftand and practife thofe Rules, believed all your Stories; why do you refufe to believe ours?

When any of them come into our Towns, our People are apt to croud round them, gaze upon them, and incommode them where they defire to be private; this they efteem great Rudenefs, and the Effect of want of Inftruction in the Rules of Civility and good Manners. We have, fay they, as much Curiofity as you, and when you come into our Towns we wish for Opportunities of looking at you; but for this purpofe we hide ourfelves behind Bufhes where you are to pafs, and never intrude ourfelves into your Company.

Their Manner of entring one anothers Villages has likewife its Rules. It is reckon'd uncivil in travelling Strangers to enter a Village abruptly, without giving Notice of their Approach. Therefore as foon as they arrive within hearing, they ftop and hollow, remaining there till invited to enter. Two old Men ufually come out to them, and lead them in. There is in every Village a vacant Dwelling, called the Strangers Houfe. Here they are placed, while the old Men go round from Hut to Hut acquainting the Inhabitants that Strangers are arrived, who are probably hungry and weary; and every one fends them what he can fpare of Victuals and Skins to repofe on. When the Strangers are refresh'd, Pipes & Tobacco are brought; and then, but not before, Converfation begins, with Enquiries who they are, whither bound, what News, &c. and it ufually ends with Offers of Service, if the Strangers have Occafion of Guides or any Neceffaries for continuing their Journey; and nothing is exacted for the Entertainment.

The fame Hofpitality, efteemed among them as a principal Virtue, is practifed by private Perfons; of which *Conrad Weifer*, our Interpreter, gave me the following Inftance. He had been naturaliz'd among the Six-Nations, and fpoke well the Mohock Language. In going thro' the Indian Country, to carry a Meffage from our Governor to the Council at *Onondaga*, he called at the Habitation of *Canaffetego*, an old Acquaintance, who embraced him, fpread Furs for him to fit on, placed before him fome boiled Beans and Venifon, and mixed fome Rum and Water for his Drink. When he was well refresh'd, and had lit his Pipe, Canaffetego began to converfe with him, ask'd how he had fared the many Years fince they had feen each other, whence he then came, what occafioned the Journey, &c. &c. Conrad anfwered all his Queftions; and when the Difcourfe began to flag, the Indian, to continue it, faid, Conrad, you have liv'd long among the white People, and know fomething of their Cuftoms; I have been fometimes at Albany, and have obferved that once in feven Days, they shut up their Shops and affemble all in the great House; tell me, what it is for? what do they do there? They meet there, says Conrad, to hear & learn *good things*. I do not doubt, says the Indian, that they tell you so; they have told me the same; but I doubt the Truth of what they say, & I will tell you my Reasons. I went lately to Albany to sell my Skins, & buy Blankets, Knives, Powder, Rum, &c. You know I used generally to deal with Hans Hanson; but I was a little inclined this time to try some other Merchants. However I called first upon Hans, and ask'd him what he would give for Beaver; He said he could not give more than four Shillings a Pound; but, says he, I cannot talk on Business now; this is the Day when we meet together to learn *good things*, and I am going to the Meeting. So I thought to myself since I cannot do any Business to day, I may as well go to the Meeting too; and I went with him. There stood up a Man in black, and began to talk to the People very angrily. I did not understand what he said; but perceiving that he looked much at me, & at Hanson, I imagined he was angry at seeing me there; so I went out, sat down near the House, struck Fire & lit my Pipe; waiting till the Meeting should break up. I thought too, that the Man had mentioned something of Beaver, and I suspected it might be the Subject of their Meeting. So when they came out I accosted any Merchant; well Hans, says I, I hope you have agreed to give more than four Shillings a Pound. No, says he, I cannot give so much. I cannot give more than three Shillings and six Pence. I then spoke to several other Dealers, but they all sung the same Song, three & six Pence, three & six Pence. This made it clear to me that my Suspicion was right; and that whatever they pretended of Meeting to learn *good things*, the real Purpose was to consult, how to cheat Indians in the Price of Beaver. Confider but a little, Conrad, and you muſt be of my Opinion. If they met ſo often to learn *good things*, they would certainly have learnt ſome before this time. But they are ſtill ignorant. You know our Practice. If a white Man in travelling thro' our Country, enters one of our Cabins, we all treat him as I treat you ; we dry him if he is wet, we warm him if he is cold, and give him Meat & Drink that he may allay his Thirſt and Hunger, & we ſpread ſoft Furs for him to reſt & ſleep on : We demand nothing in return *. But if I go into a white Man's Houſe at Albany, and ask for Victuals & Drink, they ſay, where is your Money ? and if I have none, they ſay, get out, you Indian Dog. You ſee they have not yet learnt thoſe little *good things*, that we need no Meetings to be inſtructed in, becauſe our Mothers taught them to us when we were Children. And therefore it is impoſſible their Meetings ſhould be as they ſay for any ſuch purpoſe, or have any ſuch Effect ; they are only to contrive *the Cheating of Indians in the Price of Beaver.*

---

* *It is remarkable that in all Ages and Countries, Hoſpitality has been allowed as the Virtue of thoſe, whom the civiliz'd were pleaſed to call Barbarians ; the Greeks celebrated the Scythians for it. The Saracens poſſeſs'd it eminently ; and it is to this day the reigning Virtue of the wild Arabs. S. Paul too, in the Relation of his Voyage & Shipwreck, on the Iſland of Melita, ſays*, The Barbarous People ſhew'd us no little Kindneſs ; for they kindled a Fire, and received us every one, becauſe of the preſent Rain & becauſe of the Cold.

To the Royal Academy *of* * * * * *

GENTLEMEN,

I Have perufed your late mathematical Prize Queftion, propofed in lieu of one in Natural Philofophy, for the enfuing year, viz. « *Une figure quelconque donnée, on demande* » *d'y infcrire le plus grand nombre de fois* » *poffible une autre figure plus-petite quel-* » *conque, qui eft auffi donnée* ». I was glad to find by thefe following Words, « *l'Aca-* » *démie a jugé que cette découverte, en éten-* » *dant les bornes de nos connoiffances, ne* » *feroit pas fans* UTILITÉ », that you efteem *Utility* an effential Point in your En-quiries, which has not always been the cafe with all Academies; and I conclude there-fore that you have given this Queftion inftead of a philofophical, or as the Learned exprefs it, a phyfical one, becaufe you could not at the time think of a phyfical one that pro-mis'd greater *Utility*.

Permit me then humbly to propofe one of that fort for your confideration, and through you, if you approve it, for the ferious En-quiry of learned Phyficians, Chemifts, &c. of this enlightened Age.

It is univerfally well known , That in di-
gefting our common Food , there is created
or produced in the Bowels of human Créatures , a great Quantity of Wind.

That the permitting this Air to efcape and
mix with the Atmofphere , is ufually offenfive
to the Company , from the fetid Smell that
accompanies it.

That all well-bred People therefore , to
avoid giving fuch Offence, forcibly reftrain the
Efforts of Nature to difcharge that Wind.

That fo retain'd contrary to Nature , it
not only gives frequently great prefent Pain ,
but occafions future Difeafes , fuch as habitual Cholics , Ruptures , Tympanies , &c.
often deftructive of the Conftitution , &
fometimes of Life itfelf.

Were it not for the odiously offenfive
Smell accompanying fuch Efcapes , polite
People would probably be under no more
Reftraint in difcharging fuch Wind in Com-
pany , than they are in fpitting , or in blow-
ing their Nofes.

My Prize Queftion therefore should be,
*To difcover fome Drug wholefome & not
difagreable , to be mix'd with our common
Food , or Sauces , that shall render the natural Difcharges of Wind from our Bodies ,
not only inoffenfive , but agreable as Perfumes.*

That this is not a chimerical Project , and

altogether impoſſible , may appear from
theſe Conſiderations. That we already have
ſome Knowledge of Means capable of *Varying*
that Smell. He that dines on ſtale Fleſh ,
eſpecially with much Addition of Onions ,
ſhall be able to afford a Stink that no Company can tolerate ; while he that has lived
for ſome Time on Vegetables only , ſhall
have that Breath ſo pure as to be inſenſible
to the moſt delicate Noſes ; and if he can
manage ſo as to avoid the Report , he may
any where give Vent to his Griefs, unnoticed.
But as there are many to whom an entire
Vegetable Diet would be inconvenient , and
as a little Quick-Lime thrown into a Jakes
will correct the amazing Quantity of fetid
Air ariſing from the vaſt Maſs of putrid
Matter contain'd in ſuch Places , and render
it rather pleaſing to theSmell, who knows but
that a little Powder of Lime (or ſome other
thing equivalent) taken in our Food , or
perhaps a Glaſs of Limewater drank at Dinner , may have the ſame Effect on the Air
produc'd in and iſſuing from our Bowels ?
This is worth the Experiment. Certain it
is alſo that we have the Power of changing by
ſlight Means the Smell of another Diſcharge,
that of our Water. A few Stems of Aſpara-
gus eaten , ſhall give our Urine a diſagreable
Odour ; and a Pill of Turpentine no bigger
than a Pea , ſhall beſtow on it the pleaſing

A ij

Smell of Violets. And why should it be
thought more impoſſible in Nature, to find
Means of making a Perfume of our *Wind*
than of our *Water?*

For the Encouragement of this Enquiry,
(from the immortal Honour to be reaſona-
bly expected by the Inventor) let it be con-
ſidered of how ſmall Importance to Mankind,
or to how ſmall a Part of Mankind have
been uſeful thoſe Diſcoveries in Science that
have heretofore made Philoſophers famous.
Are there twenty Men in Europe at this Day,
the happier, or even the eaſier, for any
Knowledge they have pick'd out of Ariſtotle?
What Comfort can the Vortices of Deſcartes
give to a Man who has Whirlwinds in his
Bowels ! The Knowledge of Newton's mutual *Attraction* of the Particles of Matter,
can it afford Eaſe to him who is rack'd by
their mutual *Repulſion*, and the cruel Diſten-
ſions it occaſions ? The Pleaſure ariſing to
a few Philoſophers, from ſeeing, a few
Times in their Life, the Threads of Light
untwiſted, and ſeparated by the Newtonian
Priſm into ſeven Colours, can it be compared with the Eaſe and Comfort every Man
living might feel ſeven times a Day, by
diſcharging freely the Wind from his Bowels?
Eſpecially if it be converted into a Perfume:
For the Pleaſures of one Senſe being little
inferior to thoſe of another, inſtead of plea-

fing the *fight* he might delight the *fmell* of thofe about him , & make Numbers happy , which to a benevolent Mind muft afford infinite Satisfaction.   The generous Soul, who now endeavours to find out whether the Friends he entertains like beft Claret or Burgundy. , Champagne or Madeira , would then enquire alfo whether they chofe Musk or Lilly , Rofe or Bergamot , and provide accordingly.   And furely fuch a Liberty of *Ex-preffing* one's *fcent-iments* , and *pleafing one another* , is of infinitely more Importance to human Happinefs than that Liberty of the *Prefs* , or of *abufing one another*, which the English are fo ready to fight & die for. — In short , this Invention , if compleated , would be , as *Bacon* expreffes it , *bringing Philofophy home to Mens Bufinefs and Bofoms*.   And I cannot but conclude , that in Comparifon therewith , for *univerfal* and *continual UTILITY* , the Science of the Philofophers abovementioned, even with the Addition , Gentlemen , of your « *Figure quelconque* ». and the Figures infcrib'd in it , are , all together , fcarcely worth a

FART-HING.

CONTE.

IL y avoit un Officier, homme de bien, appellé *Montrefor*, qui étoit très-malade. Son Curé croyant qu'il alloit mourir, lui conseilla de faire sa Paix avec Dieu, afin d'être reçu en Paradis. Je n'ai pas beaucoup d'Inquiétude à ce Sujet, dit Montrefor; car j'ai eu, la Nuit derniere, une Vision qui m'a tout-à-fait tranquilisé. Quelle Vision avez vous eu? dit le bon Prêtre. J'étois, dit il, à la Porte du Paradis, avec une Foule de Gens qui vouloient entrer. Et St. Pierre demandoit à chacun de quelle Religion il étoit. L'un répondoit, Je suis Catholique Romain. Hé bien, disoit St. Pierre; Entrez, & prenez votre Place là parmi les Catholiques. Un autre dit qu'il étoit de l'Eglise Anglicane. Hé bien, dit St. Pierre, entrez, & placez vous là parmi les Anglicans. Un autre dit qu'il étoit Quaker. Entrez, dit St. Pierre, & prenez Place parmi les Quakers. Enfin il me demanda de quelle Religion j'étois? Helas! répondis-je, malheureusement le pauvre Jacques Montrefor n'en a point. C'est dommage, dit le Saint, — Je ne sçais où vous placer; mais entrez toujours, vous vous mettrez où vous pourrez.

LES MOUCHES

A MADAME HE--S.

LES Mouches des Appartemens de M. F--n demandent Permiſſion de préſenter leurs Reſpects à Madame H--s, & d'exprimer dans leur meilleur Langage leur Reconnoiſſance pour la Protection qu'elle a bien voulu leur donner,

Bizz izzzz ouizz a ouizzzz izzzzzzzz, &c.

Nous avons demeuré long-temps ſous le Toît hoſpitalier dudit bon Homme F--n. Il nous a donné des Logemens gratis; nous avons auſſi mangé & bu toute l'Année à ſes Dépens ſans que cela nous ait couté rien. Souvent quand ſes Amis & lui ont épuiſés une Jatte de Ponch, il en a laiſſé une Quantité ſuffiſante pour enivrer une centaine de nous autres Mouches. Nous y avons bu librement, & après cela nous avons fait nos Saillies, nos Cercles & nos Cottillons très-joliment dans l'Air de ſa Chambre, & nous avons conſommés gaiement nos petites Amours ſous ſon Nez. Enfin nous aurions été le plus heureux Peuple du Monde, s'il n'avoit pas permis de reſter ſur le haut de ſes Boiſeries Nombre de nos Ennemis déclarés, qui y tendoient leurs Filets pour nous prendre, &

qui nous déchiroient fans Pitié. Gens d'un Naturel & fubtile & féroce, Mélange abominable ! Vous, très-excellente Femme, eutes la Bonté d'ordonner que tous ces Affaffins avec leurs Habitations & leurs Piéges feroient balayés ; & vos Ordres (comme toujours ils doivent être) ont été exécutés fur-le-champ. Depuis ce Temps-là nous vivons heureufement, & nous jouiffons de la Bienfaifance dudit bon Homme F‑‑n fans crainte.

Il ne nous refte qu'une Chofe à fouhaiter pour affurer la Permanence de notre Bonheur; permettez-nous de le dire,

Biχχ iχχχχ ouiχχ a ouiχχχχ iχχχχχχχ, &c.

C'eft de vous voir faire déformais qu'un feul Menage.

THIS FACSIMILE EDITION OF
THE BAGATELLES FROM PASSY
HAS BEEN DESIGNED FOR
THE EAKINS PRESS BY EDITH
MCKEON, PRINTED ON CURTIS
RAG BY THE STINEHOUR PRESS
LUNENBURG, VERMONT & THE
MERIDEN GRAVURE COMPANY
MERIDEN, CONNECTICUT AND
BOUND BY RUSSELL-RUTTER.